STORIES
&
THOUGHTS I

The Thinker

George Manus

Other books written by George Manus Manus

THOUGHTS,   English
TANKER,   Norwegian

REFLECTIONS I,   English
REFLEKSJONER I,   Norwegian

REFLECTIONS II,   English
REFLEKSJONER II,   Norwegian

REFLECTIONS III,   English
REFLEKSJONER III,   Norwegian

A WOMAN'S MANY MIGRATIONS,   English
EN KVINNES MANGE FLYTTINGER,   Norwegian

STORIES & THOUGHTS I   English
HISTORIER OG TANKER I,   Norwegia

INNOVATIONS AND CREATIONS,   English

70 YEARS IN COMMUNICATION - about the MAX MANUS Companies,
English

WORDS FOR THE ROAD - ORD MED PÅ VEIEN I   Eng. Norw.
WORDS FOR THE ROAD - ORD MED PÅ VEIEN II   Eng. Norw.
WORDS FOR THE ROAD - ORD MED PÅ VEIEN III   Eng. Norw.
WORDS FOR THE ROAD - ORD MED PÅ VEIEN IV   Eng. Norw.
WORDS FOR THE ROAD - ORD MTD PÅ VEIEN V   Eng. Norw.
WORDS FOR THE ROAD - ORD MTD PÅ VEIEN VI   Eng. Norw.
WORDS FOR THE ROAD - ORD MED PÅ VEIEN VII   Eng. Norw.
WORDS FOR THE ROAD - ORD MED PÅ VEIEN VIII   Eng. Norw.
WORDS FOR THE ROAD - ORD MED PÅ VEIEN IX   Eng. Norw.
WORDS FOR THE ROAD - ORD MED PÅ VEIEN X   Eng. Norw.

You are heatedly welcome to quote from this book, respecting the
copyright.

ISBN: 9788743014140

Author: George Manus
Copyright: George Manus
Design and layout: Ole Praud
Illustrations: Laura Hamborg

Printing:
BoD - Books on Demand, Norderstedt, Germany

Publisher:
BoD – Books on Demand, Hellerup, Denmark
http://bod.dk

George's online book store - www.georgemsnus-books.com
The Art of George Manus online store - www.georgemanus.com
George's Innovation & hub website - www.maxmanusinnovation.com

George Manus e-mail: info@georgemanus.com

December 2023

Version 2

Preface

This book is a continuation of my REFLECTIONS I - II and III, but instead of carrying on to number IV, it has been given a new title: "STORIES & THOUGHTS I". It is published in a smaller format and has half the content, while the style is kept the same.

I have dedicated the book to the thoughts, as nothing can be written without thoughts being involved.

Read the reflection "Thoughts" from page 7.

"Thoughts are duty free" it is said. It is important to stick to that. It's a privilege we all have as humans. All thoughts you have can be kept to yourself, and no one will ever get to know what you are thinking about if you wish to keep them to yourself.

To me, the thoughts are like steam in a pressure cooker. Especially when it comes to thoughts that I've been thinking about for a long time. They want out in one form or other and out they normally get. But, fortunately, it only applies to those I don't want to keep for myself.

I thank Anne Schild for her help with the language, Laura Hamborg for her illustrations and my friend Ole Praud for his consultancy work.

The picture of the sculpture on the first page is Le Pensure, The Thinker, created by Auguste Rodin.

The South of Spain
December 2023
George Manus

CONTENTS

THOUGHTS

October 1995

Are they just there or do we do something to make them appear? My experience is that it's difficult to keep them in order, and that has probably something to do with concentration.

My thoughts race past in a constant flickering motion. When I put it like that, it's because I feel that there is a marked interaction between my thoughts and the visual image on my retina. I've never asked anyone else if they feel the same way.

It's a wonder that one's thoughts don't boil over at times, but where would they go if they did?

One does, however, feel at times as though one's thoughts are like steam in a pressure cooker. Especially when they are thoughts one has brooded over for a long time. They want out in one form or other and out they normally get.

Can for instance a burst of anger be the actual safety valve for a collection of aggressive thoughts?

If one is totally relaxed and just lets one's thoughts flow, which thoughts get priority, and which ingenious system does the prioritizing?

Is this were the subconscious comes into it? Is it just another storehouse for thoughts?

Is it so that if one doesn't consciously suppress certain thoughts, one will be left with an even distribution of the different types?

It is undoubtedly a lot more pleasant to conjure up the good thoughts, than to struggle with a predominance of bad ones. The latter can easily become a great strain if it happens over time.

The question is if it can be so easily controlled.

Here I believe it's important that one in oneself is reasonably balanced and that one has a platform to stand on, which isn't too slippery and which gives one's feet a good grip.

Thoughts are tax-free, it is said. It's important to take note of that.

It's a privilege we all have as human beings, that we can keep our thoughts to ourselves.

No one will ever get to know what you are thinking about, if you want to keep it to yourself.

To share one's thoughts with others can be good.

How often don't we say: "Think of the time". Here one refers to thoughts about something or other, which one assumes the person one is addressing has shared or heard about.

When one experiences someone reading one's thoughts or when one feels that one can oneself read someone else's thoughts, it's probably more random or a result of being closely connected to the person and thus able to read his or her body language.

In connection with thoughts, I come to think about how good I feel right now. Lying here relaxing after a hot bath and giving my thoughts a free rein.

Thoughts
It's said that "Thought are duty-free".
Luckily so, otherwise I would be a poor man.
April 2019

Thoughts II
When you tumble with Thoughts they are normally both good and bad. Let your Thoughts flow freely when that happens, blockages can cause flooding.
May 2019

Thoughts and steam
Thoughts can be like steam in a pressure cooker. Out they shall in some form or other and out they come.
October 1995

ANTIPATHY AND SYMPATHY

Mars 2017

Antipathy, originating from the Latin "Antipathia" cannot in my opinion, stay alone. Being aware of one's antipathetic feelings, one will automatically also be aware of the sympathetic ones. Antipathy and sympathy are in other words linked together.

It is difficult to imagine that one can find anyone not being conscious about both these feelings. Not even one day will pass when we don't weigh these feelings up against each other, consciously or unconsciously, I believe.

Even if that shouldn't be correct we often have a black and white attitude to these two feelings. Either you feel sympathetic or unsympathetic towards a person. We quickly form an opinion which seldom changes, or is given a chance to change, especially if the starting point initially was unsympathetic.

It is rather unusual that one, after feeling unsympathetic towards someone, makes an approach to test one's perception?

Her comes the question, why Antipathy - Sympathy? Why not Unsympathetic - Sympathetic?

Both in English and Norwegian we use the expressions Sympathetic and Unsympathetic. But in English, unlike in Norwegian, a likeable person isn't normally called sympathetic but pleasant and an unlike-able one isn't unsympathetic but unpleasant.

Antipathetic, as far as I understand after this, is not the opposite of Sympathetic, which could be Unsympathetic. One never hears anyone say about someone else that he or she is Antipathetic. No, I believe "Antipathy" must have to do with feelings, described as feelings of discomfort or reluctance towards a person or situation.

Sympathy is described as one's ability to express feelings of sorrow towards other people due to their problems or suffering.

I suppose we all have the right to exist on this planet and that is as it should be, but then it must also be right to express ones Antipathetic and Sympathetic attitudes.

Fortunately, in most democracies one can express one's opinions about anyone without consequences, if one otherwise respects the rules of democracy.

Unfortunately, it's easy to feel Unsympathetic towards some people and Sympathetic towards others. From that point of view each of us are right, as it is our own opinion it's all about. I believe one rarely says to someone that one feels Unsympathetic towards him or her, as it's much easier to let others know one's opinion about it.

It's much easier when it comes to the Sympathetic side. "It was said or done in sympathy" or "I sympathise with your thoughts and attitudes".

It's natural that one sympathises with those with the same opinion as oneself, and if that's right it's for that reason frictions occur in daily life.

In the political world, it's logical for antipathy and sympathy to play a considerable role. Here one believe one get the whole person "served on a plate". As looks - attire - body language - expression and not least the message are all presented at the same time.

There are many impressions to be digested, which leads to one's antipathetic or sympathetic attitude towards the person.

When I say, here one believe one get the whole person "served on a plate", it's of course because in addition to the external and oratorical characteristics, a sea of unknowns are hidden in all of us. These characteristics we handle, control and use according to our ability and personality.

If you, after having read the above remain with an antipathetic attitude to this reflection and a feeling of discomfort, reluctance and disgust towards it, then you have my full sympathy.

But of course, I appreciate if someone sympathises with my reflections about Antipathy - Sympathy.

THE BAR COUNTER

2018

I have never been of the kind to hang around bar counters, but it does not mean in any way that I throughout my life have been avoiding alcohol. This story has very little to do with what is normally served from a bar, but in all modesty with the very physical part where the goods are usually served from, namely the bar counter.

I grew up on Landøya in Asker outside Oslo where my mother and Max started a life together after the war. Together with my mother I joined the moving load after she was divorced from my English father and moved to Landøya with Max. For me, it was an exciting and special upbringing with Max as a stepfather. Alcohol was a natural part of their lives, but my story tells nothing about that.

My start in first grade of primary school took place in Ulvik in Hardanger, one year earlier than usual, at the age of six. I lived with Mum's sister, Aunt Kari, after I was "kidnapped" from Sweden on June 12th, 1945.

Then, as mentioned, I moved to mother and Max in Asker and took the rest of primary school at Holmen School. With that behind me I went to secondary school from the age of fourteen, the first year at Solvang and the last two at Asker secondary school. When the class moved to the new school, each of the desks were carried by two students all the way, a distance I estimate to be close to tree kilometres.

There is no way of hiding that I've been an early starter most of my life, which may have had its background in my somewhat messy upbringing where it was necessary to use all kinds of tricks to keep going. Not least, was this the case when I started my second class at Holmen primary school, as mentioned one year earlier than usual.

With an English father and a mother from Bergen, I was born in England in 1939 and shortly after sailed to Bergen with her. Then I spent the next few years of my life in Ulvik in Hardanger with my aunt Kari and her children, Ida, two years older than me and, Per, four years older.

From Ulvik the trip went to Sweden, more specifically Stockholm, where I spent a couple of years before I was kidnapped and again ended up in Ulvik with Aunt Kari.

As one understands, this was during the war and many conditions were unusual for both children and adults. I only choose one example from that time, which may, along with plenty of others, have helped make me who I am.

I could barely have been four years old before cousin Per got me into a very difficult situation. It was probably not the first time, but this episode I quickly understood went too far.

In one of the big snowdrifts formed by the plough each side of the road that passed the house where we lived, we had made a snow cave where we could stay and where there was a little hole or window facing the road. Per had probably not had the whole plan ready, but he knew that the pompous voluminous priest, which he for some reason didn't like, each Sunday on his way to church would walk past our house. His name was Ole Johan, with a surname which is of no importance to this little story.

Per had over a period thought me a very short sentence that just had to remain between the two of us. No one else had to hear it until he said so. Authoritarian as he was and about four years older than me, it was understood that the secret was to be kept between us.

It must have been a Sunday when he in the morning whispered to me that today was the day. At a certain time, we crawled into the snow cave and sat down waiting. For what? I didn't understand anything. After a while, Per told me that when I saw the priest pass the little opening, that was the key to shouting out the sentence loud and clear. No problem for someone like me, of course, so I was sitting there waiting after Per had made it out and disappeared.

Then, after a while I heard footsteps, and when the pompous and voluminous priest walked past the opening, at the top of my lungs I shouted: "Ole Johan prestefaen". (Priest of Satan)

Such an episode can make you grow older quickly. I am not going into detail about what happened after the priest had hit the roof of the snow cave with his stick so it caved in, and then pulled me out. I don't remember the details that followed, of course, and that's probably good, but the story went all over the village for a long time.

Enough about that episode. The result of my first time at aunt Kari's, my stay in Sweden and then back to my first school year in Ulvik, made me, from my first day in the second grade at Holmen primary school, understand that I had no other chance of surviving than to confront the bullies. The reason being that I could not speak anything but a mixture of the Ulvik dialect, which is difficult enough for anyone to understand, and Swedish. This was a totally unknown and new dialect which must have been difficult for anyone to understand.

What I lacked in strength I compensated for by my quick reactions, and as time went by I got along with most of the other pupils.

Later, the language became a minor problem, and I like to believe that I ended up being close to popular, if not among the teachers, at least with most of my fellow students.

After having finished primary school, albeit with the lowest grades apart from handicraft subjects and gymnastics, the secondary school period began at Solvang in Asker in 1953.

In primary school I had been tested for what was then called word blindness. Dyslexia had not been invented in those days, I think, and it was found that not everything was as it should. When I read aloud in front of the class, which was part of the Norwegian lessons, only every other line came from the book. The rest was pure fabrication according to teacher Rimol, but that was only discovered by those who followed the text in their own books. It was said that the content was presented both loud and clear in an understandable context.

Well, not the best starting point for the next phase of my education. History and geography, apart from carpentry, were the only two subjects I had some interest in. Bible history lessons I was already partially excluded from at an early stage, having stated that it was not possible for any living creatures to stand on a column for thirty years without food. I have not checked into it, but it was presented to us as an excerpt from the Bible as far as I remember, and it should be believed.

This became a long introduction before mentioning the bar counter, but that's often the way it goes when you sit down with the pen in your hand letting your thoughts flow.

I 1952 the old main house at Landøya where we lived got an extension with three bedrooms upstairs and the entire lower floor arranged as a basement with a fireplace, a sofa with two chairs and a small table as well as a ping pong table.

For some unknown reason, when mother and Max were away travelling, and I had the house full of friends, I got the idea that something was missing in the basement. Their trips were often related to the company's activities.

At this time, I had a drum set and played together with some friends at parties. There were also a few public performances, but we were not in any way at a level that suggested we were competent for it. The set of drums was normally situated in the basement, which was the only place in the house where I could practice. As I was often alone at home with my sister and brother, we had a good opportunity to romp around at the highest decibels down in the basement. Luckily, our maid, Boddi, lived in the neighbouring house and was always understanding when it came to my gatherings as long as strict discipline was followed and the house was cleaned afterwards.

In the old house there was also a fireplace with a seating area and with a big old rose painted peasant cupboard on the opposite wall next to the door to the garden.

Except for the three large drawers at the bottom of the cabinet, the upper part was used as a bar counter. When the doors were opened, and the desk flap was let down, one had ample space to arrange both glasses and other accessories. Three solid shelves were decorated with a wide range of different bottles, all of which could be reached within an arm's length.

From my youth at home I do not remember that there was ever any alcohol abuse, but there is no doubt that the bar counter was diligently used. Nor can I hide that I, at quite a young age, did more than just sniff the cork. I don't think this was ever discovered, but Max had a liberal attitude towards alcohol and allowed me to try some wine early on.

It was the apple wine that he himself experimented with in the basement. At Landøya we had a large apple orchard with all sorts of apples. Normally these were picked into sacks and sent to the juice factory in Lier near Drammen. Back then, you got apple juice in bottles. Max had acquired large wicker covered glass demijohns and it was in these he experimented with the apple wine. I soon understood that the art was to avoid that what was to become wine was transformed into vinegar. Unfortunately, it happened occasionally, but as Max's knowledge increased, it happened less and less. But, oddly, sometimes and for no obvious reason, it happened. I cannot remember that I was ever punished for it, so presumably no one discovered that sometimes a few litres disappeared from the demijohn and was replaced with a mixture of water and vinegar.

After a while, it was not so exciting for me to continue, as the apple wine was anyway too sour for my taste. However, many of the parties with my friends received an extra boost thanks to Max's wine experimentation.

It must have been the impression this bar cupboard made on me, which inspired my idea of surprising the family with a new piece of furniture in the cellar.

What I had not been blessed with as far as theoretical school abilities went I made up for when it came to practical matters and had therefore long since passed the stage when cutting boards and nesting boxes were interesting.

The thought matured, so one day I took courage and asked the teacher if I could make a bar counter. I loved everything that had to do with carpentry, and that I think he understood, but a bar counter of all things ……. The question was hanging in the air for a long time before he answered. He did not reject the thought but explained in a nice way that this was so special that he had to take it up with the teacher's council. What was said behind those walls I, of course, don't know, but not long afterwards I was told that my wish had been approved. Additional materials had to be paid for, but otherwise there were no obstacles except that a sketch first had to be presented and approved. It was all arranged, and I was on my way.

The bar counter was to be placed in a corner of the basement and was therefore seen from above, half curved. It was to be pulled a little further along one of the walls, automatically making an entry between the wall and the bar on the other side. This way I avoided making a door. On the inside I was going to make two solid shelves, the size of the counter top.

My brother, whom I consulted regarding this reflection, thought that the whole front was made of standing bamboo. Bamboo was probably not available in Norway at that time, but he is right about it looking like bamboo, as the front consisted of half-round upright strips of wood two to three centimetres wide.

The total length must have been over three meters and when it was finally finished, Max had to collect it. It was quite a sight when the teachers were standing outside the school waving when the great American DeSoto, with the bar counter on the roof, drove out of the school yard and down Solvangveien.

I don't think that the bar counter ever became a gift for mum and Max which was the original thought, however, it kept it's natural place in the corner in the basement for several years and participated in a number of parties with both big and small guests.

What happened with it later no one can remember, and now the old house has been taken over by the third generation and the basement room converted into a corridor, two bedrooms and a bathroom.

If the Guinness Book of Records had a list of the youngest carpenters of bar counters, I would probably be quite near the top of that list.

OBSERVATIONS FROM A TRAIN WINDOW

Juni 2018

On June 17th 2018 we are on a train standing at the station in Mérida, Extremadura, Spain.

Today it's only 37 degrees, while there were 42 degrees in Seville yesterday when we boarded the train "Al Andalus", one of the classic old editions from the time when traveling by a train like this was a very special experience for the ordinary citizen.

Our trip will take us from Seville in Andalucia in southern Spain to Madrid, equivalent to a 4 to 5 hour drive by car I believe. We will spend 5 nights on the trip, all in our own suite that is intended for this. Most of the meals are also to be taken on board in special carriages equipped with kitchens. If you wish to relax, two carriages are comfortably furnished with chairs and sofas for this purpose. They also arrange entertainment of different kinds after dinner.

Overnight we slept comfortably at the train station in Zafra, a small town in the interior of Extremadura. From there it was only an hour's trip to Mérida, undoubtedly more famous and a bit larger than Zafra.

It was at the train station in Zafra I got the inspiration for this reflection. I should mention that after yesterday's 42-degrees experience in Seville and close to 40 degrees in Zafra, unlike the other 46 passengers, and due to my wife's rehabilitation after having had a stroke, we chose not to participate in the excursion that was arranged to see the city sights and have lunch at a special restaurant. We stayed on the train while this was happening and was served our lunch in our suite, after which my wife took a nap while I was sitting there meditating while observing what might happen on the platform outside. The sun is burning down from a cloudless sky, while the air conditioner in the suite is working at full speed. We have not discovered how to set it properly, because it either gets too cold or too hot so it must be turned on and off according to how we feel.

There is only one track between us and the station building, whose restaurant is opposite my window.

Only two people are to be seen, one of whom is sitting on a bench to the right of the restaurant, on the platform itself. The other one is standing just one meter away from the other and it's obvious that they are arguing. The platform is shaded from the sun by a roof that covers its entire width, which of course helps when the temperature reaches 40 degrees.

Both are, without being discriminating, I think what can be called obese. I can hardly see if the person standing, like the one sitting, is a man. The dialogue goes back and forth with arm and body movements more than a quarter of an hour before a policeman strolls over to them, exchanges some words and disappears back to where he came from.

Whether it was caused by the policeman's words or not I cannot say, but the man sitting suddenly rises, embraces the person standing and they exchange a kiss on the mouth. Then they slowly go to the restaurant door and enter. Through the windows I can see that they are sitting at a table close to the exit.

There is no one on the platform except for the same policeman's renewed presence and disappearance.

After a while, the two came out of the restaurant, moving slowly back to where they previously resided, after which the situation repeats itself. The one on the bench and the other standing just one meter away and again in full argument.

One can easily speculate about what is being debated, but it really does not matter. The scene itself gives rise to speculation.

For almost half an hour, they remain in the same position, one sitting on the bench and the other standing. Then the sitting person suddenly rises and gives the other an open-handed slap across the face, after which he quickly gets back to where he had previously been sitting. The person standing remains standing in the same position and the arguing continues. After a while the reconciliation kiss is repeated, and the policeman again enters the scene.

I have still not discovered whether the person standing is a male or a female. Everything is peaceful and after a while the policeman accompanies them over to the glass elevator that takes them down to the lower level, so that they can walk through a tunnel and take the corresponding elevator up to our platform.

After a while, they come strolling toward my window and sit down on a bench. Now it suddenly occurs to me that the person who was standing earlier is a woman, although I must admit that good will is required to see it. There they sit for about a quarter of an hour before they get up, embrace each other and return each other's kisses before they go back the same way and disappear into the station building.

We are now well into the afternoon and during this period there have been no other people on the platform than these three performers. But then after a few minutes the other 46 fellow passengers appear, all clearly worn out and overheated from the excursion in Zafra.

After everyone is well on board and have settled down, the next stage of our trip begins, which after a little more than an hour brings us to Mérida, undoubtedly a more famous and bigger city than Zafra. Here the train is stationed the same way as in Zafra, with the same image from the suite window as there, with a couple of platforms and a station building. Apart from the name and the surroundings it is difficult to distinguish the one station from the other.

After the late afternoon and evening, with a delicious dinner and subsequent accommodation, a new day appears, still with the same view from the suite window.

Like yesterday it's already well above 30 degrees when we take our breakfast at 8.30 and with yesterday's heat fresh in mind, we make excuses for not participating in the daily excursion, as it was also based on visiting Mérida's sights on shank's pony, a decision we luckily took, as it turned out that the scale also today, approached 40 degrees.

For us, the procedure turns out to be the same as yesterday's. A lovely lunch served in the suite, after which my wife is having her rest while I'm sitting by the window meditating, only interrupted by the need to switch the air condition on and off.

Unlike the station we came from, here it is full of life both outside the restaurant and on the two platforms. To get people from one to the other, they are equipped with the same type of elevators as in Zafra, seemingly working none-stop.

Trains come and go. If not so often, enough for scene changes when passengers disappear into them while new ones who have got off become visible on the platform as the train leaves the station.

The first thing I notice are all the mobile phones taking pictures of our train set with its characteristic old carriages and with a total length of something like fourteen of these. Everyone knows that this is a rare visit of the "Al Andalus" train.

As my wife and I are the only passengers on board now and my wife is having a nap while I am sitting at the window, I undoubtedly become the most photographed person on this trip.

Newly-groomed people live in their own world, whether they are waiting for the next train, or for the parting kiss in those cases where only one of them is going on the train. Some a bit more discreet than others while there are those who attracts special attention due to too much selfishness.

A young lady, who already half an hour ago as we were having our lunch in the suite had seized a bench, has changed her lying down position a lot of times, with or without her little backpack being used as a pillow. Some of her positions I notice, have gradually become more provocative than the others, but I wouldn't know, of course, if this is done on purpose or not. She's decently dressed, but without a scrap more than what's necessary for that description. She is fully aware that I'm sitting at the suite window having a full overview of everything that's going on.

After the next trains arrival and short stay, and subsequent exit from the station, the bench is empty.

A family consisting of mum, dad and three children, one of whom is in a stroller, stand by the elevator arranging their four rolling bags around them. As the elevator shaft is of glass it is easy to keep track of the five with their luggage when they burst into the elevator and disappear down under.

Minutes later, the other elevator on our platform appears, and I count more than ten people scrambling out in full confusion. It's obvious that here it's a matter of being first. The family with the stroller lost the battle and came out last. Once out on the platform and having got both the stroller and suitcases in order, one of the kids suddenly gets an impulse. He grabs the stroller with the little one and starts running between the people on the platform. Mum and dad react with appeals and gesticulations before ordering the other boy to stand guard over their luggage, before they start running after the stroller. Naturally I hear nothing of what is being said or shouted, but the scene speaks for itself.

I have often thought that it is strange that there are no more accidents than there are, with people falling onto train tracks, being subjected to the undisputed supremacy of the locomotive's power.

People make way for the two runners, but nobody seems to stop the "refugee". Not that I could see any trains coming, but with the large number of people on the platform it could not be long before one arrived.

The closer the parents came to the stroller with the little one, the faster the boy ran while the four-wheeler swung from side to side to avoid collision with the waiting passengers.

I had to push my face up against the window to ensure myself that it all ended well.

Only a few minutes later the next local train entered the station. Just a few passengers got off, after which the platform became almost empty as the train disappeared from the station.

With this and many other observations from the suite window, it's also time for me to take a relaxing afternoon nap.

Afterthought: *The headline of this reflection might have been "Observations from a special train window". The window itself was, of course, quite ordinary and not in any way special, but just because it was a window in the "Al Andalus" train, we spent long hours at the stations. Normally we would also have joined the excursions if it hadn't been for the condition of my wife.*

Here one can use the expression: *"Every cloud has a silver lining".*

ABOUT HAVING REGRETS

June 2018

In general, you regret more about what you have not done than about what you have done.

How often have you not shied away from doing something you have had the opportunity to do, found excuses that in reality had nothing to do with the opportunities themselves?

First, my little snippets about to regret, which I put on paper in 1994.

> *I regret very little of what I have done,*
> *as luckily my memory's quickly gone.*
> *I regret more what I didn't get done,*
> *all of which would have been second to none.*

> *Gave people chances – from near and far,*
> *always kept the door ajar.*
> *Yes, it has often been very dear,*
> *and hasn't always got out of low gear.*

> *A tougher stand with demands and decisions -*
> *would that have been the road to greater expansion?*
> *Undoubtedly short term but therein lies the strength,*
> *of those who know their profession at length.*

> *One needs practical experience and time to roost,*
> *maturity, effort and lots of boost.*

About having regrets I wrote as mentioned in 1994, or around 25 years ago. At that time, I was already 55 years old and quite aware of the meaning of the term.

For more than 35 years I had been responsible for everything from 25 to close to 200 people employed by the Max Manus companies.

When I begin "About having regrets" with; "I regret very little of what I have done" and ask myself in retrospect if it is still correct, it is clear to me that it was. Even in the last 25 years since the responsibility was turned over to the third generation, I believe there is little of what I have done that I have regretted.

The reason for that, however, is not because "as luckily my memory is quickly gone". Admittedly, I become as the years go by a little more forgetful, but that's not why; "I regret very little of what I have done".

In this context, it is about suppressing it, by not thinking about things that weren't much to be proud of. In other words, I feel that I probably should have regretted things more often than I have done without mentioning any examples. Possibly you get a little humbler as the years go by.

The fact that I wrote that: "I regret more what I didn't do" is clearer to me. Not because I think that what I should have done "would have been second to none", but because I too often compromised. I too often chose balanced solutions over challenges, to avoid confrontations.

If this was an expression of cowardice or a belief in better progress, I have, of course, got an opinion about, but if it's a valid one, is doubtful.

Whether I was right when I: "Gave people chances - from near and far", I probably doubt even more. The disappointments compared to the joys, were often difficult to swallow and there is little doubt that "it has often been very dear".

I am not at all convinced that those who were given chances really realized that that was what was happening to them or if others perceived it as just bolstering up.

Man is the worst enemy of man, as many of you will agree upon, so here there's a loot of food for thoughts.

That the processes that follows in the aftermath of giving people chances has often been very dear and "hasn't always got out of low gear", there is little doubt.

Especially in business time is money and then it is easy to understand that this kind of "education" can be costly.

When it comes to: "A tougher stand with demands and decisions - would that have been the way to greater expansion"?, my attitude today is quite consistent with what I wrote.

That returns in the short term undoubtedly would improve significantly, I believe.

As I at that time looked at conducting business, there was never a short term-profit. Long-term equity was in the driver's seat.

Seen from that angel, solidly and strength come with "those who know their profession at length". "one needs practical experience and time to roost, maturity, effort and lots of boost".

As one sees, the concepts of long-term business life are not the same today as in those days, something I will not regret having avoided going further into in this reflection.

THERE IS ONLY ONE WAY

April 2018

In Norway we have a saying which goes like this: "There it's no shame in turning back". This saying is mostly related to the rules of the mountain code, which says that to be overly brave while being outdoors in nature isn't advisable.

In this context I don't mean showing braveness, but to tackle adversity in a positive manner. To the extent it is possible to look ahead it's advisable to do so. To prepare for the challenges one expects to face.

If one for some reason has encountered a situation where the challenges are building up, looking back is of no help, that only leads to unnecessary and negative brooding. Of course, it's important for the sake of experience to make up one's mind about whether one could have influenced the course of what led to said adversity. This is however when the brooding should stop. Having reached this point, one should look ahead again.

Little if anything in this world is totally black or white, and that, of course, also applies here. The starting point for looking ahead and not back must be based on realism, and preferably not only on "hope". Apart from that it is also extremely important that one focuses on the major lines of development along the line ahead. One shouldn't get caught up in the minor but still unavoidable downturns that one encounters along the way. One should, of course, pay attention to them, but leave them behind as quickly as possible.

Why do I refer to the minor but still unavoidable downturns one encounters along the way? A downturn to me sounds negative, doesn't it? Why not try with: "the minor but still unavoidable uphill situations one encounters". We will all at times face uphill situations when looking ahead. If the uphill situation feels very steep and challenging or is easier to deal with, often depends upon one's own psychical and mental state at the time, but it can also be influenced by making every effort to turn it into something positive. Positivity is probably the best driving force to keep going, together with will. Will as an ingredient when looking ahead is second to none. If one doesn't have the will it is almost the same as saying: I give up. In this context it's easy to remind oneself that the first letter in will is a W.

To be a Winner. This positive word also begins with a W, and that's what it's all about. "To Win by overcoming one's challenges".

In this context it's only you who can Win.

That one gets the best possible treatment is a must and something which depends of those involved. In addition, help and support from those around you is essential, of course, but again, it's only you and the way you deal with the challenge which determines in what condition you get through it.

I wrote this reflection on the 15th of April 2018 during a stay at the Hospital Virgin del Mar in Almeria in Southern Spain.

In this case my wife was the patient, while I, which is customary in Spain stayed with her and slept on the sofa beside her bed.

Without going into details regarding the reason for her stay, I am of the profound opinion that we both share the view mirrored in this reflection, and that she is ready for all the challenges which may lie ahead.

THE SENTENCE

Midsummer Eve 1995

Then you sit there months, yes, years have passed in uncertainty

Quite understandable, when one consider the procedures necessary to investigate all aspects of the bankruptcy. No problems with that, everything has been conducted in an honourable fashion.

The only challenge in this case is that it's personal, in fact very personal.

The situation is, that when the banks ran into the big crises, after it started the 19.10.87, they quickly caught all their customers in a, perhaps not so unnatural but sly, iron grip.

Those who didn't want to play by the new rules were left out of the game.

The new rules meant, that in order to stay in business, one had personally to guarantee all credits, if not, all dealings with the bank would cease - end of story. So, what do one do at a time like that?

Does one close, let one's employees go, after they've put their trust in the Company for years, thus saying good-bye to a nearly fifty-year-old business?.

I'm of the opinion today, that the future generations of my family should choose to close if they were faced with a similar situation. I hope that they, at least in a case like this will take lesson from my experience.

Nothing was, however, more natural for me at the time, than to sign on the dotted line.

And now I am sitting here in the afternoon of the Midsummere Eve, having just arrived from abroad, with the accumulated post in front of me.

Meetings and correspondence regarding one's personal surety have now reached the stage were a final answer is in the air and a sentence is about to be passed.

Seven letters, together with about half a kilo of promotional material, is lying on the side-table.

Volvat medical centre with offer of new and improved emergency services and home visit program. Bank National de Paris with the heading: why on earth change your bank due to a random letter in the mail? Could be an interesting question after I've been through the post.

Kreditkassen, C post, third class mail, offering better service for their customers by creating a central customer register for the group where I as customer will be included. A license from the Data protection Agency has been obtained. A C5 envelope with hand-written name and address. "Fifty years have passed since we had our first day of school, welcome to our party celebrating the occasion on, Saturday the ......" Incredible. A copy of the class photo on the invitation. The telephone bill from Telenor, and Gjensidige insurance Company's statement for the 1994. A little late perhaps but I don't dwell on it.

And then it's there, the last envelope, A mail from the Kredittkassen.

Your surety for the involvement in....

Am I happy that they're only asking for additional information relating to the case?

Was I not before opening the envelope prepared for the final sentence to have been passed?

Am I relieved?

It is difficult to express emotions when waiting for a verdict.

A NOT UNUSUAL DAY

24 mai 2018

Are you are looking for details in the depth, this heading could apply for a lot of days here in the South of Spain where, if one is observant, it seems a lot are a bit special for a person raised in the north. One gets surprised that here the pendulum turns fully to both sides.

If you have ordered a craftsman to a certain time on a specified day or accepted a delivery at an agreed time of something that has been purchased, one should assume that the day in question may as well be written off for other purposes.

I must however, admit that this has become far better over the last 20 years I have lived down here as a retired.

I hurry to mention that Andalucia is probably somewhat special in many ways and surely not representative for the rest of Spain.

Either you get a phone just before the car arrive, precise on time, or if you are lucky, a message that the turnout or the delivery is not going to happen at the designated time. Or you hear nothing at all.

A typical example having nothing to do with this little story, but which may be significant in terms of deliveries, I have lately been able to observe at several instances.

In short, I regularly receive samples or small deliveries of my books from Germany. The shipments take place either by mail or by DHL. If it happens by mail, it's okay if the shipments are made to the correct address, our mailbox. If it happens with DHL, such packages can't be delivered to a mailbox, so if that's the case I have an excellent deal with the local restaurant in the urbanization.

With the tracking number I can follow the movement of the package. This works great, but lately I get completely incomprehensible information. DHL informs that a special appointment for a new delivery time has been agreed with the restaurant, so obviously it is about a delay.

Of course, no agreement has been made about delayed delivery time, so in this case it must be DHL wanting to have their back clear statistically when it comes to delivery at the right time, as deliveries in this case will always be correct according to their documentation.

Well, we know that it is in the Spaniards blood to "take a Spanish one." Whether this is a statistical fraud that covers the world in general in this giant company, I have no idea, but it is nearby to think that this method isn't a Spanish invention.

Anyway, today, this Monday, I start with a trip to the bank. There are a couple of bills to the paid to the publisher in Denmark and I must also have a signature on a life certificate about my pension. Furthermore, the newspaper, which my wife is reading every single day, will be picked up.

Usually we take these tours together and combine them with some general purchases and a cup of coffee on the road.

My wife has had a stroke six weeks ago, so it's me cooking, purchasing and otherwise following up what is needed. At present, the most important thing is that the blood pressure is recorded at specific times and that medicines are taken at the right intervals. Everything seems to go well, but it's not to be denied that the nerves are going a bit on edge these days.

To ensure that the whole morning is not spent on a bank visit, it's important that one get there early. The housewives are queuing up immediately after their men has gone to work, and the late visitors will be leaving for home again at time to start cooking for lunch. Siesta-time is normally from 14:00

to 17:00 and the banks close at 14:00. The bank branch I use opens at 8.30 with limited capacity, and as mentioned above, the big influx occurs after 10:00.

Having had breakfast and made the kitchen ready for lunch, I drive the quarter it takes to the bank.

The branch, at the time I arrive at 9.30, is served by two people. Apart from a few customers, it's only me present, so I'm breathing relieved and approach the female attendant who is free.

Usually, I am waiting to be served by Maria, as she for a long time knows everything about my banking transactions and is used to doing them. She has not yet started her working day, so it takes some time for the attendant to understand how to do the transfer to Denmark.

After a while, she gives up and, as the bank still only has a few customers, she introduces me to her male colleague whom I had previously contacted when Maria had been too busy. He completes the assignment with the transfers and then signs and stamps the life certificate.

So far everything just fine. Assignment number one is completed in just under half an hour.

New fifteen minutes' drive to the store selling my wife's newspapers and magazines. The young lady serving this, has clear instructions every day to reserve "El Mundo", Spain's conservative main newspaper, as well as certain magazines and supplements she has ordered.

The shop is located right next to Victor's cafe bar, where we often take our morning coffee after having picket up "El Mundo" plus. Today, I'm alone and take the opportunity to visit the ATM machine, which is only a hundred yards away from Victor's.

I prepare the card to draw 300 Euro from my account. In Spain, they have also started closing the bank branches, and this one which we have used for a long time disappeared about a year ago and now only the ATM machine remains.

I notice that the English text on the screen doesn't exist anymore, it's limited to Spanish.

Because I'm helpless when it comes to operating any kind of dispensers I'm doing something wrong, which causes me to receive a receipt for the withdrawal, but without receiving the cash. After some time, where patient souls behind me became increasingly stated, I resigned.

Passing Victor's on the way back to the car it comes to mind to show the receipt to Victor, as we have known for many years, to hear his opinion about what's happened. He is in no doubt that the receipt showed that 300 Euros was drawn from the account, and recommends that I immediately visit the nearest branch for a clarification.

The town of Vera, ten minutes later. I find myself a parking-place outside the bank branch, not far from the closest parking machine. Two parking officers are standing beside it, and since a metal door in the machine is open, I understand that something is going on. True, the machine is out of order. When asked about where the nearest machine is, I understand that he means one which is much further away than the one I can see across the street. My first thought is to try that one first. Large white paper sheet indicates that it's "Fuera servicio", out of order.

Now my patience was exhausted, so I went straight to the bank and approached the attendant I recognized from previous visits, which I could see was in conversation with a colleague. I present the receipt and explains in my rusty Spanish: This is the receipt for having received 300 Euro, but my wallet is empty. Less than a second after I've shown her the card, she explains that I have pressed the wrong key and that the operation has been cancelled.

She then refer me to their ATM machine and suggest I try it. A little easier at mind, I ask for 300 Euro and everything goes perfectly until I, for the first time in all years I have used a card, can see that I am charged 10 Euro in commission.

What did I do wrong this time I thought.

Back to the first attendant, who quickly refers me to another. With a smile, she explains that I have pressed Credit-card instead of Current account, so the commission was rightly charged.

I Soon realized that it was an extensive operation to correct the fault and left the bank with smiles and good wishes. From possibly being around 300 Euro poorer, everything was now limited to around 10.

Back on the street, for one reason or another, I'm thinking about how relatively little noise it was in the otherwise crowded bank and took me to the ear. No, it's not possible, have I in all the changes between the usual glasses and reading glasses, managed to lose my hearing aid?

What have I done wrong to deserve such a fate I think again and hurry to the car. The only thing missing now to complete the morning is just a parking fine.

I expect to be believed if I now tell that the ticket was under the windshield wiper, but fortunately it was not the case.

The hearing aid was acquired after the old, five months ago, disappeared with my suitcase, which was never found after a flight with Norwegian from Copenhagen to Alicante. That story, which is the worst customer treatment I have ever witnessed, I made a reflection about which you will find on page 78 in this book.

Luckily, I found the hearing aid in its special box at home, and the blood pressure returned to a reasonable level. It is enough that one of us has the challenge of keeping it in place these days.

It's correct that the title of this reflection is "A not unusual day", because in his part of the world there is hardly a single day without unforeseen events occurring.

However, you should not regard them negative, as you don't stiffen in your life as a retired.

EVOLUTION

May 2018

In the reflection "Revolution" in my book REFLECTIONS III, I used a few examples of technical revolutions and evolutions.

In this reflection, it's about the slightly more vibrant part. The one about how life in general, having first been created somewhere, and over time been spread to other places, and for some to the whole globe.

I have the feeling that this phenomenon today is presented as if it is a revolutionary new discovery. The only difference is that we today are scientifically aware of how the spread has taken place.

It can probably be discussed if the heading "Evolution" in this context is correct, because it is more about emigration than on biological development, which probably is the true meaning of evolution?

One believes to be able to prove, from different angles, how this has happened and happens.

To me, this is nothing new.

Even in my lifespan we have witnessed how different scientific expeditions believe to have proven how people have emigrated from continent to continent and established themselves in most parts of our world giving living conditions for humans.

Thor Heyerdahl, perhaps the most of well-known Norwegian outside the country's borders, has proven how people could have travelled great distances a long time before modern technology made this possible for everyone.

He has written several books, translated into 60 languages.

They tell about his various expeditions, like the Kon-Tiki raft made of balsa trees and the two reed boats Ra I and Ra II.

His most famous expedition was probably the trip from Equador in South America to the Polynesia archipelago in 1947.

After the expedition's participants had first felt the balsa trees in Equador's jungle and built a raft only by ropes and without the use of materials other than those available in the past, they spent 101 days on the 6900 kilometre voyage to the target. As an example, it is the same distance as from the South of Spain to Svalbard.

All expertise judged the expedition to be madness, and every sense indicated that it was. It was suggested that the balsa-logs would draw water and eventually make the raft sink. The claims, however, were made ashamed.

In this way, he believes to have proven that the Indians in South America could have settled Polynesia long before Columbus discovered America.

Thor Heyerdahl's expeditions were just a few of the tens of thousands of similar examples of how people have emigrated throughout our planet.

The above, which is related to human emigration, is likely to count as a trifle compared to how everything living from micro-organisms to plants and animals of all types has, from its very beginning, spread and adapted to living conditions that they were not equipped for originally.

Evolution is not something one can sit outside and describe, as one always is in it, and part of it.

ATTITUDES

2016

Without attitudes, I disregard the physical, much would look different in our world. It's probably not as if everybody has attitudes of the kind I'm thinking about, or more specifically said, conscious attitudes.

That is surely as it should be, but then it is also important that those with conscious attitudes stand for them and that may be more of a challenge.

"My attitude to that matter is". Dominant attitude, here it is about people with clear attitudes, at least in their own opinion, and they wish to express them.

Many certainly have attitudes that they in every way seek to live up to.

Those I think of do not always have to express their attitudes, they only have them, live up to them, and in view of that, they appear in the eyes of others as people with attitudes.

There are no limits to what attitudes you represent and observe with others if you think about it.

Here are some examples of twists with attitudes:

Flexible and Stretchy attitude
As Flexible, you choose solutions suggested by others - while as Stretchy, in addition, you bend down to tie the shoe leases.

Dominant and Resilient attitude
As a Dominant, you are stubbornly on your point of view while as a Resilient you adapt to others.

Strong and Weak attitude

As Strong, one emphasizes one's Strengths while as a Weak one displaces and suppresses them.

Black – White attitude

One simplifies one's views to an either - or.

Hopeless and Hopeful attitude

As Hopeless, one can see no way other than giving up while as Hopeful one strive to reach the goal.

Impervious and Influence-able attitude

As Impervious, one steer straight forward without paying attention to anything while as Influenced one consider other's ideas and thoughts.

Tolerant and Intolerant attitude

As Tolerant one is indulgent for the sake of home peace - while as Intolerant one stands out to mark oneself.

Loving and Unloving attitude

As Lovingly, one turns the other cheek around with a smile - while as Unloving one does everything to reject further dialogue.

Evil and Good attitude

As Evil, one wants others' pain and suffering while as Good one does everything to make others feel well.

Stated and Overbearing attitude

As Stated, you stretch out your arms and shake your head - while as Overbearing you smile and accept other's mistakes.

Compassionate and Insensitive attitude

As a Compassionate, one takes an interest in others' situation with sympathy while as Insensitive one rejects all approaches.

Caressing and Repellent attitude

As Caressing, one feels comfortable and want close contact - while as Repellent one clearly indicates the desire for physical distance.

Angry and Sour attitude

As Angry one reacts with strong expressions - while as Sour, one is sad and little talkative.

Friendly and Unfriendly attitude

As Friendly, one slip easily into most environments - while as Unfriendly one will be standing outside.

Moody and Humorous attitude

As Moody one appears weak in social context - while as Humorous one will be remembered as positive.

Whatever your attitudes, providing they are not bad, it's important they are genuine and that you take good care of them.

Remember attitudes are a big part of your personality.

HOLE IN ONE

September 2018

For all regular golfers, I don't think of the elite who make a living from it, the experience of hitting the hole in one stroke, directly from the tee place, is a great experience. It's an event that often is leading to the one in question having to offer drinks to all present in the bar. Quite a few golfers are insured against such an event, normally together with their golf equipment.

Considering that golf balls are only 4,267 cm in diameter and that the distance to the hole can be anywhere from 100 meters upwards and the diameter of the hole itself is only 108 mm, it appears like a miracle when it happens.

It has probably happened before, but I consider my first and only Hole in One as quite special.

I am on a golf trip with three friends to the South of France. We'll be there for a week and play golf every day, and this special day is the second time we play the Old Course Canne-Mandelieu.

The evening before, we encountered two sympathetic English couples in the hotel bar and since we had tee of time relatively early the next day, they asked if we had anything against them joining us to have a look at the facility and our start.

They were not golfers but curious about what was happening since we had talked so warmly about our golf experiences.

The next morning we were all in place at the clubhouse where morning coffee number two was taken and everything made ready for the round.

The weather is always a topic of discussion in connection

with golf. The forecast for the day was pretty good, but for us it looked far from being so. Heavy clouds hung low over the terrain, and at the first tee place the sight was not even fifty meters.

The English couple had followed us to see our first shots and were of course interested in what we would do when it was impossible to see where to aim due to the fog.

The only thing we recognised from our first round a couple of days before, were two big pine trees, which we could easily see the contours of about half way to the green and the hole.

As we were standing discussing the direction and distance to the hole, we could see that the impression our new friends had got of golf, did not tempt them to challenge the sport's nature experiences, as we had so warmly talked about.

I don't exactly remember the length of this first par three hole, but chose a four iron, so I guess we're talking about a little more than 150m.

All four have now made their shots into the fog and our friends decided to follow us to see the results of our first shots.

The next is that we pull our golf trolleys into the fog, followed by the four non-golfers who must have wondered what in the world anyone can see in this sport.

We stick to the fairway between the two pine trees, which is easy to follow, as the transition on both sides from the fairway to the so-called ruff, is clearly marked from the short cut to the higher cut grass.

Suddenly the green pops up and we see the flag located at the back of it.

No balls to be seen on the green, so everyone is spreading out to explore the area. Eventually we found three balls, all of which were recognized by their respective owners. That's why it was just my ball missing.

The grass at a wide distance around the green is not higher than we should have been able to see the ball if it was in a reasonable distance from it, but so far no ball in sight.

Suddenly one of my friends exclaim: Then there's only one place it can be.

As he reaches the flag, he points down and nods as he shouts out: Hole in One.

The most disappointing and most uplifting impression of the world of golf became our new friends experience this morning. Everything within less than half an hour.

We separated on the first hole, they with their new experiences from the world of golf and I with my hole in One.

A few hours later, after having completed the round with beautiful natural experiences, the fog had disappeared, and the sun was shining from a bright blue sky.

As I was going to report my hole in One in the club house, we were greeted with a typical French shoulder pull, followed by: Yes, and so what.

I once again got a confirmation about my opinion, already formed in my youth, about the French people's general relationship with those who don't master the French language.

Nobody showed the slightest enthusiasm for my Hole in One other than my golf friends, who thought that since I got away not spending drinks to everyone in the bar, nothing less was expected than for me to invite for lunch, of course with Champagne to be included.

The pleasure was completely on my side.

MEMORY AND MEMORY CAPACITY

Oktober 2018

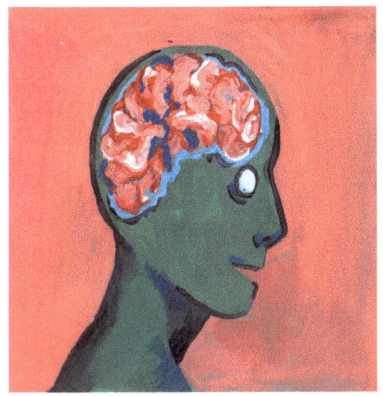

I call this reflection Memory and Memory capacity. Only after this one was written, I discovered by accident that it already exists a reflection about the Memory. It was written in April 1994, which is about 25 years ago. It's to be found in my book RE-FLECTIONS I.

I've written more than 200 reflections so far and still have a list of more than 100 headings.

How could it be that I have forgotten the "Memory." I put it on the list just a few days ago. Imagine having forgotten something as important as the "Memory". It is probably situations like this who reminds you that you are no longer as young as you were. I intentionally don't use the word - old - I prefer to describe the development towards the older years as the maturation process.

As I don't know the answer I have no coverage for it, but I wonder if we are all equipped with different memory capacity, or if it's only a matter of how the capacity is utilized?

In this context I'm not talking about measurable capacities as in the data world, as there you only expand the capacity when necessary. Anyhow, as we humans until this day are unable to increase our memory capacity it would be interesting to know the answer.

Technical progress is moving forward, and the capacity of storage media is constantly increasing, allowing opportunities for new quantum leaps in the applications.

Yes, if it had just been so easy when it came to us humans. Perhaps it will come a day when you can plug in extra memory capacity in an implanted connector for this purpose.

Well, at least, those at my age don't have to philosophize about this, we'll have to do the best we can with the capacity we have received, as we know it's inevitably weakened as we mature.

I will be 80 in May next year and have for several years noticed the need for extra memory capacity.

One continues with the capacity one has received and make oneself believe that one can remember what one wants to remember and prioritize. Maybe there's something right in that? Things one think are insignificant to one's own situation, one pushes aside with the hope that it will free up capacity for more important things.

All this doesn't happen in a calculated way of course, even if one think one is conscious about it.

Basically, I don't think this works, that is, increasing capacity in the areas one wants to remember by pushing aside things you think is immaterial, but it's a good excuse for yourself. Perhaps this method is connected to the latter, the displacement method.

The latter may not be so conscious. Some have their own ability to suppress, not to allow special unwanted thoughts to absorb capacity. For them, I think, however, that it has started early in their lives and before they became conscious of the capacity shortage in the memory. It probably has more to do with human attitudes and urge for personal protection.

Imagine that the memory, or the degeneration of it, caused you to forget about your progressively reduced ability to remember.

Personally, I have difficulty with the displacement. Perhaps it is a good sign, however, that you remember and accept that the memory is usually weakened in line with one's lifespan.

AN UNUSUAL EPISODE

23 May 2018

For special reasons, we had to make a trip to Almeria, the nearest city of any size. If you stay within the speed limits, the trip takes about three quarters of an hour, with normal traffic.

Why there were an unusually large number of big trucks on the road that day, I do not know, but I observed that that was the case. We take off from home around five o'clock in the afternoon and get the steadily sinking sun in our faces most of the time.

In the twenty years I've lived here, our twentieth wedding anniversary being yesterday the twenty-second of May, there have been numerous trips on this motorway south and southwest.

As the trip is to the hospital we belong to in Almeria and it's a visit in connection with my wife's stroke almost six weeks ago, the talk logically is about this topic.

As usual we're not in any particular hurry, I set the speed control at 115 km. per hour. And apart from the stretches where the hundred km/h limit is marked, that's my speed. According to the average Spaniard, 115 km/h is the speed of "domingeros", which refers to "Sunday drivers" and the 100 km/h sign, at least 90% of them ignore.

As a "Sunday driver" one's driving rhythm becomes completely different and requires special attention to avoid getting into trouble. As a "Sunday driver" you also have to focus extra on the rear-view mirror, as it is incredible how fast a car going in 160-170 km/h comes upon you when you're driving in 115. The speed limit on the Spanish motorways is 120 km/h.

49

That's precisely why so much time goes by keeping track of the traffic coming from behind. What I'm about to describe now I observe in the rear-view mirror.

On a long stretch of several heavy transporters, which in this case, unlike usual, are keeping a reasonable distance between them, I see two or three passenger cars in the right-hand lane. In front of them, the left-hand indicator lights start flashing on a heavy transporter as he glides over to the left lane to pass his colleague in front of him.

These heavy carriers have a speed limit of 100 km/h, and must be said to generally follow this limit. Probably, it is because they are provided with logs that could get them into trouble if speeding. Had that not been the case, they would probably like most Spaniards pay no attention to the speed limits. The two cars behind the overtaking lorry, also move into the left lane at a reasonable distance from the heavy transporter.

Probably, for the log not to detect speed violations but that, of course, I don't know anything about, the overtaking lorry keeps to the maximum speed, which is more or less the speed of the lorry he passes. For this reason, it takes more than half a kilometre before the overtaking heavy transporter has passed. He, however, remains in the left lane after overtaking instead of moving over to the right lane. Fortunately, the road in front of me is clear, so I look more in the rear-view mirror than forward when I notice this occurrence.

The overtaken lorry now pulls in between the two cars following the overtaking lorry in the left lane, and I see that he turns his lights on, even though the sun is still shining.

The two cars then turn into the right lane and drive past the two combatants on that side.

After they have successfully overtaken the combatants to their right, the overtaken lorry starts flashing all its front lights. As far as I could see he was just a few meters behind the overtaking lorry when he starts to move from lane to lane.

I suppose he was on his way home to Andalucia with empty cargo space, after delivering vegetables somewhere in Europe, since the lorry swayed dramatically from side to side by his manoeuvre.

Had it been fully loaded, it would probably have overturned.

This stretch of the motorway is the longest straight bit of the whole trip so I could follow the event for several minutes. All the traffic behind them had no chance of passing the two giant "highway gladiators".

Latin temperament "Yes", but as you will understand a little later on in this reflection, I'm careful to express my opinion about it, as I myself can at times become very excited by many daily events.

The result of our visit to the cardiologist was that we immediately should take new blood tests and report back in one week to make adjustments to the medication.

Today is Thursday the 24th of May. It's the day of the week when our cleaning lady comes, and the day when my wife's blood test is to be taken at a clinic in Vera, just six kilometres from home.

We are lucky to find a parking place close to a parking machine, at around nine o'clock.

As far as I know, one Euro covers one and a half hour's parking. I have the Euro in my hand and let it disappear into the slot of the machine. After a bit of trickling, it appears where the change normally arrives, without any sign of a ticket.

Nothing new, the reflection "An unusual morning" on page 33 of this book also deals with parking in Vera, so that is not unknown.

After several attempts without the parking machine being willing to swallow the Euro and give me a ticket instead, I give up.

I am happy my wife is sitting in the car. For a long time, she has been tired of hearing me cursing about what I call idiocy so I head across the street to the next parking machine I spot in the area. Here the same thing happens. The temperature is rising and now it's very good that my wife is still sitting in the car.

As it is a matter of getting to the clinic early to take the blood test, we give up getting a ticket and hurry to the clinic.

In the waiting room there are already eight or ten people and following the Spanish custom one asks one of them: Quin es el ultimo? which means: Who is the last one? That way, one clearly knows when one's turn comes. Excellent system when there are no numbers to be pulled or other means to control the queue.

While sitting there waiting, some newly arrived people go straight to the door of the doctor's office. After a while we understood that their errand was to collect their tests. From previous experience, we also knew that it's not necessary to collect them in person if you master the internet as they can be downloaded online.

Today it turns out that the person who takes the samples doesn't have an assistant, so there are never-ending interruptions after interruptions and, of course, a lot of unrest among the waiting patients.

Enough said, a good half an hour later it became my wife's turn and when she was in there two such interruptions happened.

After she was told that they would call when the test was ready, something they estimated would happen in the morning before we in the afternoon had to go back to the cardiologist at the hospital, we take the lift down and get back to the car.

As in most other places down here, the efficiency is high when it comes to enforcing the parking rules.

And so also this time, under the windscreen wiper, I find a special envelope with some printed matter stuck into it. Could it be an apology for the parking machine being out of order? On the contrary, the envelope was a kind of parking ticket. So, one was to be punished because the technology had failed.

I utters some strong words in Norwegian. My wife knows them, of course, and shakes her head in resignation, while I give her the envelope and ask her for a suggestion as to what we ought to do with it. She has not previously seen this form of "punishment", so in the first instant we decide to do nothing. and drive the five-six kilometres to the store where the newspapers are purchased.

With the newspapers in hand, we walk over to Victor's and order coffee and a "tostada con tomate", or toasted bread with tomato. My wife had to take the blood-sample before eating, so for that reason we had skipped breakfast at home.

Only now we take a closer look at the envelope. All that was written was, of course, only in Spanish, a language my wife masters better than her native French, but which I find little meaning in when written.

Four Euro and thirty cents were to be put in the envelope as a penalty for the machines being out of order. Probably completely logical according to the Spaniards, but what should one do with the envelope? We ask Victor's son Jake, who serves us, if he is aware of this form of "punishment". Yes, he was, although he had no personal experience never having got one of them, but had heard from someone else hat the envelope with the money was to be delivered to the bank. Never ever had I heard anything so stupid but we must not forget that we are living in Andalucia.

From Victor's we drove another five or six kilometres to Mojacar to buy flowers. Some friends gave my wife a big bouquet of yellow lilies when they learned that she was home from the hospital.

These beautiful flowers last only a week, so now we renew them continually when the old ones have done their job.

While I was buying the flowers and getting back to the car, my wife had called one of the two numbers that were stated on the envelope. She had talked to a male person who said that if we drove back to Vera, just well over ten kilometres from where we were, we should call him again and arrange to meet him, so he could explain what we had to do.

Throughout this period, I had quite strongly expressed how I felt about the different "specialities" one has to deal with when living in southern Spain, so the atmosphere between us was highly charged. It went so far that she clearly stated that it would be my fault if she got another stroke.

We didn't exchange many words on our return trip to Vera. There we found a parking space in about the same place as before and saw that around both parking machines plenty of people were gathered, discussing and gesticulating. Apparently, the machines were still out of order.

My wife tries to put a new call through to the person she had talked to before, without getting any response.

In her condition she should of course, not have been part of any of these events, but it was not easy either, or rather, it was impossible to stop her.

Suddenly I saw a parking attendant wearing an orange top, and suggested he was the person to consult. He was walking around placing envelopes behind all the windscreen wipers. It was not easy to convince my wife about it, as she was still determined to make the telephone contact as agreed upon.

I soon ran out of patience and took her by the hand over to the attendant, who strangely enough was not overrun by desperate car owners.

The only thing resulting from the conversation with the attendant was that he insisted that 4 Euros and 50 cents should be put in the envelope. Not as it said 4 Euros and 30 cents. We had already put 4.50 in it and told him so.

Satisfied, he put our envelope in his pocket and continued his task of supplying the cars with envelopes under their windscreen wipers. I could not resist shouting a few abusive words about the parking agency in general at him. I don't accuse him of anything, but I strongly doubt if the money in the envelope was ever entered into the account books.

Either way, we had, in our opinion, done all we could to settle the matter, and returned to the car. There it was parked without a new envelope, something we had unknowingly prevented by turning to the very person who was supposed to put them there.

My poor wife was completely exhausted and went straight to bed when we got home.

Little by little I calmed down, and while my wife was resting I started doing some work relating to my writing.

I made a Skype call to my contact in Denmark, who helps me with the technical issues of publishing, and, of course, I briefly mentioned the current episode to him.

To my great surprise, he told me that when he visited our place a couple of years ago, he had a similar experience. At that time, they had found out that the envelope with the amount indicated had to be put through a purposely made slot somewhere on the parking machine.

So, in the future we will know what to do if it happens again.

The next day I checked out a parking machine, and found a tiny letterbox slot about ten centimetres above the ground.

I conclude this reflection by mentioning that, of course, I realize that it's wrong to call the envelope a parking ticket and a punishment. As you have parked, you have to pay for it, but how they have arrived at the cost of 4 Euros and 30 cents, I can't help wondering.

IN THE SPIRIT OF DEMOCRACY

14 Juni 2016

The word democracy means parliamentary rule.

The people in democratically ruled countries decide the policy to be conducted. The political party having the majority, either formed by its own voting, or by coalitions, largely determines the policy to be conducted if the constitution is followed.

Democracy was developed in Greece 500 years before Christ and is used as a form of governance in most western countries and in more and more countries around the world.

In the spirit of democracy, we must, with the freedom of governance that it is meant to give us, make provisions.

We are free to decide which party to vote for, which in principle means that we support the idea that we are all in principle equal, a form of government intended to give freedom, but which takes all people under one comb. In other words, having as a manifesto that everyone in principle is equal and consequently should share the benefits of society.

No problems with that side of democracy. If this form of governance, as practiced by some socialistic parties, had the prerequisite to work, I think even I would sympathize with it.

There is only one small problem with sharing the wealth, and it is first and foremost: where does it come from and who created it?

Then, what about sharing the many negative consequences that occur when the wealth suddenly doesn't exist anymore? The cash has run out because of low motivation, general downturns, or lack of incentives created for the creative powers.

Most importantly, in my opinion, is to find the answer to:

Where did the wealth come from and who created it?

What percentage of the population believe that economy means that there exists buckets full of money which could be shared between us all? Maybe simply phrased, as fortunately, fewer and fewer believing it's like that.

Moreover, unfortunately there are many meaning, and often with justification, that some manage to get much more than others. Probably correct, corruption happens everywhere and not least here in Spain.

As far as I understand, Spain is topping the list in Europe in this context, but in all fairness, they're working hard to get to the bottom of it. But, as with all ingrained habits, it takes time to get rid of them.

Greed is indubitably a bad thing and of course there are many in society who, without social responsibility, abuse their position to enrich themselves. It is unfortunately a natural consequence of human nature and proves that we are in no way equal.

In nature no animal would survive if it wasn't the strongest and best in the tribe that became leaders. A democracy in the animal world would probably lead to extinction.

Maybe we would be vice to dwell more about that?

If everyone is to decide, presumably the only justified form of governance, society will slowly but surely stop if one doesn't open for compromises. It must be acceptable that some are better than others to create, and that they, under responsibility, must be given stimulating and motivating conditions. Many democratic societies, fortunately has understood this.

In today's democracies, individuals can decide which political segment they want to belong to. In this way one obtains affiliation and has a platform from where to express opinions, and thus achieves a social safety.

How many political segments, or parties, a democracy might consist of is determined by the citizens of the democracy. Anyone is free to form one's own political party. If one reaches the given minimum votes, one is in progress.

It is morally correct that no one, "without consequences", should enrich themselves on the expense of others. Just the little "without consequences" is the most important thing, because it is unfortunately in many people's nature to try and let the morals sail in its own sea.

Are leaders with the ability to fill the buckets, equally good at leading the community? Without arguing for or against, I believe that's not the case. Protecting wings spread throughout society, and the considerations that must be taken to ensure all, do not belong to those making every effort to achieve financial success.

Possessing diplomatic skills and having studied all the rules and regulations of bureaucracy, does not give any guaranty for you being a good leader and far from you having financial flair. In this context the black and white rule does not necessarily apply.

Speaking of contradictions and accepting that it is so, it is only logical to accept that both extremes are necessary conditions for the community to function. Both extremes must be stimulated to do their best.

Tolerance, balance and compromise are important factors in this context.

Regarding the politician, I go along with Nelson Mandela's definition: Politicians want their ideas to stay alive.

The more people deciding, the more bureaucrats are needed to investigate and clarify all different views. Bureaucracy is costly and the bigger it becomes the more complex and expensive it gets. By the very nature, bureaucracy itself creates a continuous need for growth.

It is hard to imagine a democracy that would work without bureaucracy. Considering all the fractions in society, the term: "The more chefs the more mess, comes to mind".

Wikipedia describes the bureaucracy as follows: Bureaucracy is a hierarchical organization of decision making where individual cases are handled by caseworkers with carefully defined decision-making authority by common rules and where all employees "bureaucrats" are responsible to management for decisions to be in accordance with the regulations. The purpose of bureaucracy is to ensure equal treatment of similar issues and a high level of detail control from management.

Bureaucratic organizational form is a prerequisite function for public administration in a democracy to work, but one also finds traits of bureaucratic organization in (larger) private companies. Emphasis on the correct procedure often leads to bureaucratic organizational form, among other things, being criticized for spending unnecessary time deciding. Therefore, the word "bureaucracy" in the daily language is usually used as a derogatory expression of cumbersome case processing.

The Irishman Edmund Burke wrote about conservatism in a democracy back in the seventeenth century:

"I believe in the essential weakness and corruptibility of human nature, in the incapacity of the average man to resolve his problems in a rational manner, in the irrelevance of most "rational" solutions to political problems".

According to Burke, the community is not a rationally constructed structure, but an organism that develops gradually.

Any attempt at radical turmoil must therefore end in disaster. The constraints of reason make it important to respect traditions and fear revolutions.

Wikipedia describes Establishment as a denomination of the dominant group or elite that holds power or authority in a nation or organization. It may be a socially closed group that chooses its own members or specific elite structures in a government or a specific institution.

Political bureaucracy also includes an elite governing and dominating.

To me precisely because, as described in Wikipedia: "The Establishment" is a denomination of a dominant group or elite that holds power or authority in a nation or organization, it can easily get a protectionist side.

Would it not be natural that those who work in "The Establishment", seek protection by sheltering themselves from the insight of us deadly? In their eyes, we are likely to be narrow-minded and to incompetent to understand the complex overall picture that concerns the governance of society.

The more complicated and comprehensive, the more shielded and insensitive becomes "The Establishment". Purpose Achieved.

Should democracy work after the definition, "The Establishment" and its bureaucracy must be made visible and accessible and attackable in one way or another.

How to do it peacefully, I have no answer, but I'm in now doubt that it is necessary.

THE RACE

Aug. 2018

What triggered me for this reflection happened an ordinary Thursday now in August. The setting is as follows:

My wife had an appointment with Nicole, a quarter of an hour's drive from home. Because she can't drive yet, due to a stroke she had a few months ago, it is me who oversees the transport.

Everything is fine, the cleaning lady comes at. 9.30, the manicure at Nicole will take place at. 10.30, and then the day's appointments are concluded with my wife's weekly rehabilitation at 12.15, before today's shopping.

I spend the waiting time while she is at Nicole, at Victor's cafe and bar, just a few steps from the entrance to her Salon, and order a lemon tea and some water. It's a little cooler today than it has been the last couple of months, the scale showed 29 degrees an hour ago on the terrace. From experience we know that it will reach 35 degrees in the middle of the day.

All tables under the umbrellas at Victor's are practically full and I still have about one hour before she finishes. With paper and pencil, I pass the time by starting this reflection.

It takes a few minutes from we sit in the car until we are out of the urbanization, and before the automatic gear-box shifts to top gear we are overtaken by a bright red Volkswagen Polo. Not more than a dozen seconds later, the distance between us must be close to a kilometre.

As Nicole, being Italian, lives in the same urbanization as us, we know her red "German" and her obvious pleasure of challenging its unconditional driving skills.

It was immediately after she overtook us, that I was thinking of another "race".

In this case, Nicole was supposed to open her Salon Favola before my wife arrived, and right enough, ten minutes after overtaking us, I can see the red car a kilometre ahead of us on the newly built motorway, as it turns into the roundabout and then into the car-park. It was only the traffic that made it impossible for her to increase the distance by several more kilometres.

My story, whose only geographical comparison is that it also happened in a Latin country, in Italy, was about a completely different setting.

In charge, and responsible for the Norwegian National Team in Skeet clay-pigeon shooting, during a major international championship, the trip went to the city of Montecatini Terme, not far from Florence. This took place once in the early seventies.

I could still make myself reasonably well understood in Italian after my school stay in Italy in 1957-58 and the whole squad had an unforgettable stay in all respects even though we didn't get any medals.

The closing dinner, where I could thank for the stay on behalf of "La Squadra Norvegese", the Norwegian National Team, in Italian, with subsequent festivities, became a special memory for all of us.

As the leader of the team, which for the most part was severely limited when it came to foreign experience, it was obviously a big responsibility for me to make everything work to the smallest detail.

The shooting took place over three days, so there were plenty of administrative activities for my part.

The team was accommodated in the same hotel, and from departure to return, all passports, tickets and as well export and import papers for the weapons were in my custody. After a little spread when the official dinner was over, everyone finally caught up in the hotel.

I had naturally arranged it all for the next morning, with early departure to the airport in Pisa. The bus was ordered and wake up calls and breakfast organized in good time - all in best order.

The distance on the motorway from Montecatini Terme to Pisa, I see today is 53 kilometres, and is considered a 45 minutes' drive. How much of the trip consisted of motorway in those days I don't remember, but I had a special experience this morning, getting to know there are several roads leading to Pisa.

With the sun directly in my face I wake up. Jumping out of the bed and checking the time, I observe that the bus, if everything had gone according to plan, should have just left the hotel.

A minute later, I find myself at the reception where the owner welcomes me with a smile. It was in no way answered with a smile from my side. Rarely, if ever in my life, I've taken someone by the collar, but just that happened. Why did no-one wake me up and where was the squad?

The fact that I had not been awakened, he made excuses for, but all the others had both eaten breakfast and now sat in the bus on their way to the airport. - All without tickets, passports and weapon licenses. The panic quickly turned into thoughts about emergency solutions.

Think of the newspaper notice on the first page of Dagbladet: "The Manager of the National Team in Clay-pigeon Shooting, fails the troop during an International Championship in Italy."

The grip in the collar is tightened, after which I make it clear that in two minutes I'm back with my suitcase and make it clear that there is only one option. He brings to the airport before the bus arrives, regardless of the choice of means.

When I again appear at the reception with my suite-case, the owner stands in the front door and winks me out to an Alfa Romeo of the type, large sedan.

The notion that all roads lead to Rome, of course, do not apply to Pisa, but never have I been passenger in a car on a regular road, exceeding the speed limit on the motorways. For the hotel owner, I think this was a challenge he appreciated and there was nothing holding back his pride when we arrived at the airport and found that no bus he knew were there.

Well out of the car with my suitcase in hand, and immediately after I had thanked him for his driving, the bus approaches the departure hall with a smiling and happy Norwegian National Team.

No one had been thinking about me. As I had not shown up at the breakfast they had all taken it for granted that I had made it to the airport in advance to receive them there and welcome them to the trip home. And it was just the latter I did.

If I remember correct, I kept the episode for myself, since nobody would be happy to know how close to a big disaster they all including myself had been:

The hotel owner with his large Alfa Romeo had won the race for me.

SANTA CLAUS

Desember 2017

Here one stands at the driving range with a selection of golf clubs, hitting one ball after another out into the empty air in the hope of getting better. For me it's not a matter of becoming a better player than the others, but to improve my own game.

Looking at my results lately, it's obvious that I should spend more time on the range than I do but bear in mind that I'm a pensioner and thus very busy with activities of all kinds.

It's not these activities which are the reason that seven weeks have elapsed since my last hair trim. Normally this happens at the same hairdresser as my wife is using down at the coast, every four weeks. I feel very comfortable with these intervals between the trimmings, and have followed this routine for years. As I don't sport neither a beard nor a moustache which also must be trimmed, the whole séance takes less than ten minutes.

The hairdresser in question is extremely popular among the ladies who frequently wish to present themselves with good-looking hair, something my wife fortunately never neglects.

The hairdresser, who is French, only employs one helper, thus being in the lucky category of having more than enough work. My wife has fixed appointments for months ahead and normally so have I.

This time, however, a logistical fault has occurred relating to my appointment, without the blame being put on either the hairdresser or my wife. I stick to my slogan that the boss, in this case me, is always responsible if something goes wrong, so we won't go into that one.

As we, at the time this was written, were close to Christmas, the consequence of the logistical fault when it was discovered, was that the four-week interval could not be upheld even if the actual time it takes for the hairdresser is less than ten minutes and that my wife is one of his best customers. The interval became seven weeks.

As I, as far back as I can remember, always like to have some discrete curls at the nape of my neck, these extra three weeks led to the hair on the side and neck reaching a completely unacceptable dimension. On top it's not so important, as I have come to terms with the fact that up there, nature as well as an advanced age is anyhow taking its toll.

The day before I finally were to sit in the barber's chair, as mentioned after three-weeks of overtime, I again visited the driving range in front of the hotel.

Without having counted them, about twenty tee places are available for anyone wanting to practice their skills in golf. To collect golf-balls from the machine one uses a card or a chip which can be bought in the pro-shop. The balls, while coming out of the machine, drop into a plastic basket which one puts in a suitable place. Each time the card is entered, or a chip is used, out come 25 balls.

As the Friday in question was sunny and relatively warm for this time of the year, most of the tee places were occupied. Having found one empty, I left the clubs I had brought with me and went to collect a basket of balls.

It turned out that Martin, the pro in Valle del Este, was instructing 6 or 8 children aged 8 to 10. Many parents were present having brought with them brothers and sisters of the hopeful, so that they could get an insight into what was going on.

Back at the tee place I prepare myself with some body movements before starting.

Both players having finished their rounds and others on their way to playing 9 holes in the afternoon, as well as guests having had or going to have a refreshment on the terrace in front of the hotel, pass by.

Many stop to have a look at us practising and discretely make comments between them about the quality of the strokes.

The first basket with 25 balls is empty and I collect a new one. The heavier tools in the tool-kit of golf clubs are now to be activated. For one reason or other it's more inspiring using the big club, the driver. In theory, anyhow, it's the one supposed to give the longest ball flight.

Back at the tee I prepare myself for the first attempt to reach the 200-metre mark. Positioning is of the greatest importance. As I'm focusing on the leg position and direction and knee flex, I can clearly hear a loud voice of a child saying: "Mira Papa – Papa Noel juega al golf". (Look daddy, Father Christmas is playing golf).

Turning around I see the little boy with his left hand in his father's right and his own right hand pointing at me.

With a big smile I acknowledge his comment by saying: "Feliz Navidad" - (Merry Christmas).

After exchanging mutual smiles father and son hurry along, while I came to think about the way I was dressed. Long yellow trousers, a golf shirt with a white collar showing at the top of a pink sweater and with a red cap on my head. Not strange that this together with my greyish white curls in the nape of my neck and wispy whiskers sticking out from under the cap, had made the boy make a comparison with Santa Claus, now that Christmas isn't far away.

I am not at all sure if the father didn't let the boy believe that it was the real Santa Claus he had met.

THE CREATORS "COMPASS"

Februar 2018

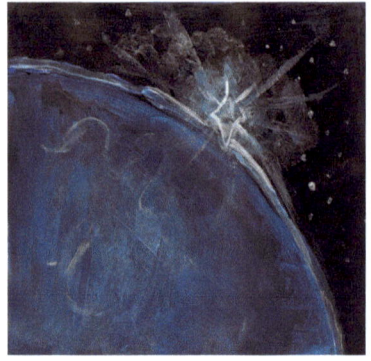

The most precise instrument I can think of is the Creator's "Compass".

Already, millions of years ago our planet, mother earth, was prepared for what was going to happen, that we, the humans, were to become the ones to build up our world the way we see it today. It was only a matter of how long it would take for the Creator to find the correct conditions and combinations to create us humans the way we are today. Far from perfect, we are probably still the race best suited to organize what we call our world society.

The evolution continues, and we have just initiated our attempt to create order within our own ranks here on our planet.

With an infinite number of galaxies in space, the specialists claim there are many hundreds of billions of them only in the part of the universe that we can observe, and with the billions of planets one today believes our solar system contains, it's clear to me that nature which I for the sake of my understanding call the Creator, must have possessed great mathematical skills.

Our planet revolves around the sun and, in our galaxy, I believe that is the basic condition for our existence. Contrary to us "incredible" creatures being newcomers on the planet, the sun has existed 4,6 billion years.

All this is of course being ruminated over by specialists in all fields related to the universe. Theses of all kinds I am sure covers this subject satisfactorily, and that is good.

Others, with minimal knowledge about this subject like me, I am sure also will have thoughts and meanings on this, although not necessary of any value to the scientists, but at least for oneself and those especially interested.

What I am most impressed about is how incredibly precise the Creator's "Compass" must have been at the time he drew up the plans from where our planet should get its energy, and in what form it should receive it to provide a basis for life as we know it.

The sun, which the Creator chose as a source of energy when he constructed our planet, sends it out in form of sun beams, which according to our time scale, uses 8 minutes and 19 seconds from when they start until they reach us.

Where I live in the South of Spain we have the Mediterranean on one side and are mostly surrounded by mountain ranges of heights from a few hundred meters up to about fourteen hundred.

Compared to Norwegian conditions, with a few exceptions, we have summer temperatures the whole year round, while we during the winter periods at times can see snow on the highest mountain tops.

From certain places one can see the snow on the mountains of Sierra Nevada, less than two hundred and fifty kilometres away, with its excellent skiing conditions quite a few months of the year. The highest peak reaches 3,478 meters above sea level.

For reasons we humans in my opinion to a limited extent are part of creating, we experience changing weather patterns, with consequences like drought and flooding.

Here we are, we pore souls on our planet, in a situation where we take actions which shall, and will, be of importance for future generations. The truth is probably that we have no ability to look further into the future.

No reason to dwell on this. That remains for the bureaucrats and politicians to sort out and that's probably how it should be.

Apart from that it's obviously important that we all consciously participate in the endeavour to protect our planet with all the means we have at our disposal.

On the Creator's drawing board, at the time our galaxy was under construction, I envisage the sun drawn as a circle.

My focus goes to the Creator's "Compass", which in one way or other must have been used. He had the sun as a circle in the centre of the drawing board at the time our galaxy was under preparation. The sharp point on the "Compass" is placed in the middle of the circle. With his divine brain, the Creator had already calculated the precise distance needed for the energy from the sun to reach our planet and to create the basis for life.

Following that he must have drawn a circle with the correctly calculated radius. This circle forms the centre of our planet which at all times will follows the perimeter of this during its cycle around the sun.

He has already drawn billions of planets belonging to our galaxy, so now he must carefully check his calculations to make sure that our planet, while travelling around the sun does not collide with others.

Precision equal to his calculations to solve all challenges while creating our universe, our scientists are, without derogation, light years away from reaching.

With the sea as the starting point and up to the highest mountain top on our planet, Mount Everest, it is 8,848 meters. Whether it's measured during high tide or low tide, I don't know, but in this context, it's probably not those details that count, and a little allowance I suppose one must leave room for.

The energy from the sun which makes life on our planet possible mustn't just be stable, it must be 100% stable. Think about the fact that the sun beams have travelled 149,6 million kilometres before hitting us without having been disturbed or delayed on the way.

Below the surface of the sea there is life - a lot of life. Not for us humans without artificial aids, but as energy for us in form of food. Isn't that a clever solution? Getting to the top of Mount Everest requires a supply of artificial oxygen.

Conditions for life for people on our planet is, without help from artificial sources, only about 8,000 meters above sea-level. It's good to know that we can move freely all over our planet without the help of artificial means, if we stay below this height.

Despite of the enormous distance the sun beams have travelled before they hit us, they have with constant effect reached us with their energy all this years, and thus made all life known to us possible.

If one takes into consideration that our revolution around the sun takes 365 days, according to our time scale that is, we should be grateful that the Creator's brain was the way it must have been, and still may be, and that the "Compass" he used, and maybe still uses when he created the universe, is an instrument of utmost precision.

One can wonder if the creation he was determined to make is finally completed, if the end mark is set, or if The Creator is still sitting at his drawing board, somewhere in the universe, creating solar systems with new life in one form or other? In that case, a development must surely have taken place also there, so maybe he today has an electronic Compass even more precise than the one he used at the dawn of time? There will be more innovations and entirety will get more complex, and of course it's important that he limits the amount of collisions.

Maybe we are so fortunate that he already has, or is about to, create life in some shape or other out there, where based on the mistakes he has already made with us humans on this planet, has abolished our bad characteristics and improved the good ones.

STOCKHOLM MEMORIES FROM 1943 - 45

2016

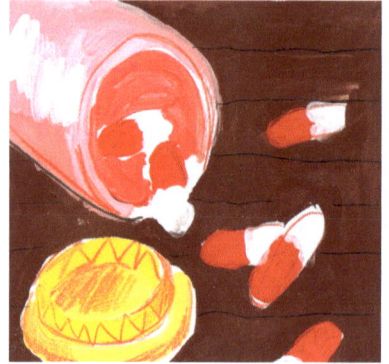

I only remember fragments of events from my stay in Stockholm during the war, and it's just two events that have really left an impression. The first one I only remember bits and pieces of, while the other I myself told the family several years later. The third one I do not remember at all, but my mother never forgot the story of the "Poison pills", which I reproduce in a short version below.

I came to Stockholm in February1943 and stayed until I was "kidnapped" on June the 12th 1945. The story about the "kidnapping" is reproduced in my book REFLECTIONS III.

This should not cover too much history, but I still must mention the reason for my stay on the eastern side of the border.

My mother married my English father George Bernardes in 1936. She moved to England, and I was born there on May the 14th 1939. It may sound a little strange that he, apart from running his family-business and being an officer in the oldest regiments in England, The Honorable Artillery Company, was transferred as a consul to the South West town of Haugesund in Norway.

The Regiment was established in 1573 and amongst other it is a part of: The 1st Intelligence, Surveillance and Reconnaissance Brigade, so it may not be so strange after all. Anyhow, apart from his consular activities I have understood that he was monitoring the German maritime movements along the Norwegian coast.

As the war progressed and the Germans occupied the country, he moved northward and ended up in Åndalsnes in the county of Møre and Romsdal, where the place he was staying got hit by a bomber. He was transferred to Ålesund Hospital, heavily wounded with metal splinters in his head.

By the Germans he was transferred via Vollan Prison in Trondheim, to Møllergata 19, a prison in Oslo, from which he was later moved to Sweden.

On the 25th of June 1941 he was operated by the well-known brain surgeon Olivecrona and became, for one and a half years, a convalescent at Badhotellet Sanatorium outside Stockholm. He later ended up as the British vice consul in Stockholm.

In his own report he writes: "It was not before May 1942, that my wife and son in occupied Norway had been permitted to join me here in Sweden, after Christmas 1942 before they learned the good news, and in February 1943 they were able to leave."

The first pedal car must for every small boy have made a big impression. So also for me. Many years ago, I phoned Gunnar Sønsteby, a famous colleague of Max's from the war, to get a clarification upon something I never got straight. I remember I got my first pedal car in Stockholm and have always had the impression that it was a gift from both Max and Gunnar. He could confirm that he, very soon after mother had started working in the British legation and he had met her there, was invited to our home in the flat. He was the only guest and had bought the pedal car as a present to me.

I seem to remember it was red, but it may be that I get it mixed up with the fact that the first pedal car my half-brother got at Landøya also was red.

According to Gunnar I had manoeuvred around the flat seeming very satisfied with the gift. In other words, the pedal car was a gift from Gunnar alone. Further on he also mentioned that he didn't feel very welcome during the visit, and that his impression was that father still suffered from his injuries.

Gunnar, who was in Stockholm on many occasions in those days thought he was the only one of "the boys" being invited to our home. As far as he could remember, Max had never been there.

Before the flat in Sandhamnsgatan 33, the number may be wrong, we lived in a little Pension, from which I only have one picture of myself in some kind of uniform.

The flat was situated in one of several blocks and from pictures I have seen, but don't possess, it was quite ordinary.

Mother could of course have confirmed if they had a piano, but now it is too late. She died in 2010. I got a feeling they had one but it may also be that I mix my impressions with later ones from Landøya in Asker in Norway, where I grew up after the war, lying under the grand piano together with our English Setter Pan spending peaceful moments there, when my mother played the Bechstein.

Back to Stockholm.

New blocks were being built close by, and because of that a big barrack for the workers was built, having two or three floors. At the specific time I am describing, no one had fortunately yet moved in.

I remember that we were several boys together, but how we happened to be there alone without supervision I do not understand. I suppose it must have happened during a weekend, as there was nobody in the area apart from us. This must have happened in 1944, which means I was 5 years old.

Suddenly, we find ourselves in a room with a big cast iron stove. For unknown reasons I must have had a box of matches in my pocket, and came immediately to think of the combination stove and matches, as being made for each other. With a lot of wood chips and plank cuts on the floor a fire was quickly lit. It must have been cold, and the plan must have been to warm ourselves.

We quite soon discovered, however, that the stove had no connection to a chimney so panic set in. The flames came out where the connection to the chimney should have been, and seconds later the wall was on fire.

Panic and mass exodus. After this, the only thing I remember is that I ran across the green grass of some football pitches. I imagine that was the shortest route to the Legation where mother worked.

I heard the fire trucks with sirens blaring and saw the barrack going up in flames far behind me. I don't think I ever had any symptoms of being a pyromaniac, so I suppose that lighting up the stove was meant to warm us up, but as mentioned, where did I get the matches from and why did I have them in my pocket?

It's strange that mother never could remember this episode. Is it possible that I managed to keep quiet about it? Well, no one was hurt but for me the smell, colour and atmosphere have stayed in my mind ever since.

Fortunately, later in life I have never had any unpleasant experiences related to fires. Just the cosiness in front of a fireplace.

I am pleased I was too young to understand anything at all about the next story, which took place in my mother's office at the British Legation. Next, I give a short excerpt, translated into English, from a chapter called "Poison pills", from her biography "Tikken Manus sabotørenes hemmelige medspiller" – "Tikken Manus the saboteurs secret co-player", which was published in 2008, with permission from the publisher. The book was never translated to English.

"I really felt very happy in my little office. It was intimate. Through the sloping window a squirrel came every day to greet me and to get some bread crumbs from my hand. I had one chair for me and another for the saboteurs that came to see me. Nothing of what was said inside the four walls was to leave it. I was called auntie by the boys from Kompani Linge. (The main resistance organisation in Norway). That was my code name and it was also the code for the safe".

To the right of her working place Tikken, mother's nickname, had a big iron cabinet. She always had to make sure that it was properly locked.

"This big, terrible looking iron cabinet also contained something I appreciated very much in those days: a shelf filled with Players cigarettes. All other items in the cabinet was directly linked to the illegal activities. I was the only one with access to the poison pills".

On Sundays, Tikken had to bring little George with her to the office, a curious little boy of three to four-year old, because then his day-care centre was closed. One Sunday he is playing on the floor as usual. He has brought with him e few small tin soldiers which he made up short stories about. Each of them gets life when he gives them voice and personality. Tikken is hammering away on the typewriter to finish the daily reports to England. It's urgent. She opens the iron cabinet and grabs a packet of cigarettes, lights one up, and continues writing. She shushes to George when he's hammering on the floor with his tin soldiers.

"Suddenly I see him standing there with a poison pill in his hand! I thought my heart would stop and that my last moment had come. My little boy with the big pink pill. Such a pill could terminate the life of a grown-up man in less than a minute. I can still see it as if it were today. It is light pink, rather big and looks like candy. It would, of course, be very tempting for a little boy. I had been careless and had only myself to blame.

To have been so careless as to have left the door to the cabinet open! I came to myself and with lightning speed, got hold of the boy and twisted the pill out of his hand as he was about to put it in his mouth."

Most probably it was only a coincidence that I didn't swallow the poison pill that Sunday in my mother's office before she discovered what was going to happen.

BOARD MEETING IN COPENHAGEN

Desember 2017

This story has nothing to do with the Board Meeting in Copenhagen itself. It's all about my special experience related to the trip home afterwards.

The outcome of the event is not known when this is put on paper. It's today about a month since I, on December 9th, 2017, arrive at Kastrup Airport in Copenhagen to fly to Alicante in Spain.

From Alicante, a two-hour drive South on the motorway will bring me home to Valle del Este, close to the town of Vera.

I am to check in on Norwegian flight 085371 departing at 11.45.

A row of automatic check-in machines are placed in the area outside the counters, where it is expected that one, after having received the boarding pass and luggage tag, shall deliver one's luggage at so-called "Baggage drop" counters.

As I know that my suitcase is considerably overweight, about 9 kilos, and as I am not at ease with these automatic check-in machines, I turn to a nearby uniformed lady who follows me to one of the "robots".

Overbearingly she asks me for my ticket and positions the bar-code under a reader – no reaction. Following a couple of attempts and after having observed that all the other "robots" are engaged, and that people are queueing around them, she claims that the "robot" in question is out of order and that I will have to go directly to the counter.

This suits me perfectly.

I was attended to by a helpful male person who immediately confirmed that my suitcase weighed 29 kilos. I was to escape, he says, by paying for 8 kilos overweight – 640 Danish kroner. Credit card ready and everything OK.

The last I see is my suitcase disappearing through the hatch behind him, with the circular round leather identification label marked Valle del Este Golf Resort – Vera Almeria, containing my personal business card.

To hours to departure according to the information board.

I make myself comfortable with a cup of coffee and my hand luggage and think back on the fifth of December, five days ago, when I flew from Alicante to Copenhagen to attend the last board meeting of the year and to spend time with my family from Oslo who, apart from my daughter and son in law, this year also included my two grandsons Nicolas and Oscar, nineteen and twenty-one. I was also to have a separate meeting about other matters, and thus arrived one day before the family.

The family business is represented in all tree Nordic Countries, thus the board meeting in Copenhagen.

The only possible alternative within the framework of human departure times was to fly from Alicante to Oslo with Norwegian, and then, after a stopover of about one hour to continue with SAS South again to Copenhagen. Quite alright, but because of the short stop in Oslo and the change of airline, I could only travel with hand luggage, as there was no chance of getting a suitcase transferred from Norwegian to SAS in such a short time in Oslo, as I had to go through the complete check-in procedure once more.

As my plan was to bring back home various stuff from Copenhagen, I was prepared to buy a new suitcase there to be sent as luggage on my flight home.

I took off from Alicante on December the 5th and had my first meeting in Copenhagen on the 6th. This meeting had to do with the status of a project in Max Manus Innovation AS.

All according to plan I arrive at the hotel after the meeting with my, beforehand emptied hand luggage now filled with heavy books whereof I am the author, and a bag containing a prototype of an electric self-driven wheel. The history of the wheel, covered in one of five chapters in my book Innovations and Creations, I will not describe closer.

The Board-Meeting in Max Manus AS was held on the 7th, followed by the traditional dinner while Friday was set aside for the family-gathering, after I in the morning, at Illume, had bought both a new hand luggage and a suitcase.

Before returning home, the original hand luggage, now filled with heavy books, as well as the prototype of the wheel, were placed in the new suitcase together with certain other items which there was no place for in the new hand luggage, as well as my toiletries which from experience would be an extra complication during check-in. This was the one that weight 29 kilos, which I a short time ago had checked in on my direct flight to Alicante.

Boarding time is approaching, and I walk to the gate. Seating is almost non-existent, so I place myself in the already existing queue. Queues are not my strongest side. I always feel unwell in queues. It didn't help to the situation that the plane was close to half an hour late. A mixture of insecurity and nausea is building up. Finally, the gates open, and each passenger gets through by using the bar-code on the boarding-pass. Seat 1A, finally there and able to sit down.

Then came the traditional recommendation over the intercom that once having found the seat one should sit down to let the others pass.

Gradually everyone has found their place, the counting has been done and both the front and the back-cabin doors have been closed.

As usual I take a quick look in the in-flight magazine, while we are backing out from the gate.

As I was flying Norwegian I wondered if the picture of my step-father was on the plane's rear tail fin, as I had had no chance to check it when boarding.

He was born December the 9th – 1914 and died September the 20th 1996. He would have been 103 years this very day.

So far, I have seen the plane a couple of times at various airports, but as far as I know, I've never flown in it.

It's comfortable in the first row at the window. In the neighbouring seats a charming Norwegian couple, my age, going to spend Christmas in Spain.

When the time comes, I order my favourite meal, beef stroganoff with rice.

As I have a couple of hours drive from Alicante, I stick to fizzy water instead of wine or beer and end the meal with a coffee.

A relaxing trip without any big events and with plenty of time to reflect on the meetings and the less formal gatherings. Landing on schedule, still light outside. Remains only to collect the suitcase, get to the car and start on the final stage.

Luckily there are relatively few people in the arrival hall, because of fewer planes at this time, and thus the luggage would arrive quicker - I thought.

Fewer and fewer passengers remained around the conveyor belt as they happily collected their suitcases and golf-sets and left.

In a flash I came to think about the events that happened five years ago. Norwegian from Copenhagen to Alicante. Only a short flash, but that story cost me a few thousand Norwegian crowns and a lot of time and aggravation thanks to some blunders in the transport system. That "trip" ended up in my book REFLECTIONS III.

Shaking off the thoughts I registered that I was almost the only passenger left. Is it possible – has it happened again?

Same procedure as last time five years ago, but this time

at a different counter for "Lost and found", dealing with the Norwegians passengers and their problems.

Impeccable service, and the lady behind the counter could immediately confirm that the suitcase was registered in the machinery in Denmark and that the reference was in order.

Formalities took place and if I called next day they would most probably know what had happened.

The follow-up from my side regarding what I call relevant supplementary information, has so far been made and automatically confirmed with relevant dates.

To make a long story short, I only mention that I first filled out a form they sent me following my first inquiry, to Norwegian "Bags@Norwegian", and returned it the 13.12.2017. The last of 3 additional pieces of information I sent Jan 3rd, 2018 and received also for this one an automatic confirmation.

Writing this, we have arrived on March 9th, 2018, exactly 3 months after the "disappearance". Not one word so far other than the automatic answers to my earlier supplementary information.

I have in these estimated the value of the suitcase and its content and today I sent a complete report questioning the state of my case and what kind of closing procedure they have for "luggage disappearances".

Another month has elapsed during which I sent several follow-ups but this time without receiving any form of answer. It is quite clear dear Mr. Kjos, (CEO Norwegian Air Shuttle) that my case is not the only one – Norwegian are probably drowning in its own incapability to organise itself.

In my time as a businessman we had a saying we called Customer Care. In those days that did not mean that the customer was only a necessary evil to achieve economic success, something I, in my experience have all reason to believe is your interpretation of the term.

I don't need to go further than reading the last edition of

our local Euro Weekly News her in the South of Spain, dated April 12, 2018. Under "Having Your Say" the heading reads: "Norwegian flies high in air transport world".

The following comments from Robert Carter and Mark Rainy respectively speaks for themselves. 1) They are worse than Ryanair for the come in, sit down, shut up routine. Very bad at keeping schedules from my experience with them. 2) They don't deserve it. Absolutely diabolical customer service.

In an interview with Bjørn Kjos in "Kapital" no. 6 in 2018, he said: "I try to travel in such way that I avoid checking in luggage". Maybe that would be a good recommendation to give his own passengers?

Further on in the same interview he states: "When working in business you must always take chances. That belongs to the strategies one chooses. If you don't dare to fail you stand no chance". Very well, but where does the customer stand in all this?

The article further explains that Norwegian communicate directly with their target audience, not the voters but the customers.

Good to know for those of us having experience with their form of communication.

The last word I have yet to get from Norwegian, but as per today, April the 14th, 2018. I choose to add the following "words for the road", which I unfortunately did not get into my last book "WORDS FOR THE ROAD III", but don't worry it will be part of the next one and thanks, Dear Kjos, as it got triggered a couple of days ago while thinking of you and your organisation:

"The business leader who doesn't put the customer first - will sooner or later have to deal with the negative consequences that follow."

The last time I heard from your machine, Bags@Norwegian, was on March the 26th. Throughout this period since the beginning of December last year, 2017, all my inquiries have been answered by a machine and I can't imagine that any human being has been involved from your company's side until I returned the submitted Lost Luggage Form as I received on that date, just days after receipt.

Even after that, I have not heard a word in response to my inquiries.

Then suddenly, on May the 9th, 1361.00 Euros appear on my bank statement.

According to the information I received on March the 26th, it would be entirely in accordance with the Montreal Convention, so Norwegian will be completely within their rights. The value of the suitcase and its content was many times the amount of the compensation transferred. Not a word has been received other than the transfer I discovered on the account statement, exactly six months after the flight.

I thank you so much.

That I was so stupid as to send valuables beyond ordinary travel effects is of course my own mistake and especially without having had separate travel insurance. The ticket was paid with a Norwegian, not your airline, credit card with travel insurance, but the insurance obviously does not apply when the traveller is resident abroad.

One should of course read the small print carefully, something that people my age probably are not very good at.

For your information, the e-mail correspondence with the robot covered 25 A4 pages when I copied it over to this reflection. Not that I thought it should follow the reflection, but maybe someone in the future might find it interesting to read about an example of how things were handled by Norwegian in 2017-18.

Life goes on, and this reflection is not about lost values in the form of earthly goods, but it's scary to detect how shaky relationships seem to have become in many everyday situations.

By the way, I must add that my own experience of the actual flights with Norwegian is completely in line with what you can expect. But again, as Kjos mentions in his interview with Kapital: "When I travel I try to avoid checking in any luggage".

Perhaps he himself has had bad experiences, and one must not forget that it is easy to blame others. It is, as far as I know, not Norwegian who hold their protective hand over luggage handling.

THE CYPRESS

2017

The first time I really discovered this stately tree, *Cupressus sempervirens – the Mediterranean cypress,* was during my stay in Italy from 1956 to 1958.

After having finished the first part of my education as a technical instructor at *Olivetti's factories in Ivrea in the North of Italy, I was transferred to their commercial school in Florence.

The address where the school was situated and where I was going to live, was Via Bolognese 106.

If I recall rightly, Olivetti had the following villas at their disposal: Villa La Pietra, Villa Coletta, Villa Sosetti and Villa Natalia, all surrounded by a truly impressive park.

The first time I came there I was standing with my mouth open. I was to stay in Villa Natalia which borders the Via Bolognese, while the lessons took place in one of the other big villas.

In all directions one could see well grown cypresses, most probably planted at the same time as the houses were built, the first one in the latter part of the sixteen hundred.

Sempervirens means that they are evergreen and can apparently be up to thousand years old and reach the height of 35 meters.

As I got settled and particularly after my Vespa scooter was exchanged for a Lancia Aprilia 1949, the weekends were used to explore the surrounding countryside.

I got my driver licence in Florence on my eighteenth birthday, the 14th of May 1957, only a very short time after coming there.

Wherever you went, starting at the school, you were always met with these magnificent majestic cypresses.

A favourite place to visit was Fiesole. You only followed the Via Bolognese farther up from where I lived, until you reached this lovely place. On the way you pass many viewpoints from where you can enjoy the magnificent city with the river Arno and Ponte Vecchio as well as the Duomo.

In this area you won't find any apartment buildings. Large mansions with gigantic wrought iron gates and with fully developed cypresses in all gardens, encircle the entire route up to Fiesole.

Of all the places I have been in Italy, this stands for me as something very special.

Strange enough, I never went back to Fiesole, even if I quite a few times have been back to the region. For all I know it may all have changed, although I very much doubt that. The Italians are clever when it comes to preserving their culture.

Fiesole is an experience all its own with among others it's antique amphitheatre. It's a place where the car is parked, and one orientates oneself on shank's pony.

Again, I can see it for me, grand cypresses in all directions. They belonged there in this environment where they majestically formed a natural part of the picture.

Tuscany, with Florence as a base, stands for me as the part of Italy I like the best. I have had the pleasure of visiting the region many times since then and can never get enough of its magnificent impressions.

Just outside the village of Greve in Chianti, on the way up to Lamole, you will find an old stately mansion called "Vignamaggio". The owners, who lived there when I last visited the place, run, apart from their wine production, a hostel of top quality.

The movie "Much ado about nothing", based on the play

by the same name, written by William Shakespeare, was shot on this magnificent location. In my opinion a very special film in the romantic genre.

The road to Lamole, which runs through this property, is built with a hedge of giant cypresses alongside it. Obviously, they were planted so close to each other that they today form a giant impenetrable wall along the whole property.

I am sure one can find similar places with cypresses elsewhere, but I have never seen any, and where else would one find such a total setting.

If it wasn't for the winter in Tuscany, which can be both cold and quite snowy, this would probably have been the place I would have chosen to spend my life as a pensioner in.

The endless undulating landscape with its characteristic villages, and with vineyards and olive trees in all directions together with scattered Mansions surrounded by giant cypresses gives the impression that time has stood still.

I can't imagine any better place in which to give one's soul rest.

Well, Tuscany thus never became my place of retirement. The climate in the South of Spain, as well as a lot of other circumstances, was the reason for my ending up there.

The remembrance of the cypresses in Italy must have made a special impression on me, as it didn't take long after the house in Cabrera in the South of Spain was built, before my wife and I planted our first cypresses. The start was a couple along the driveway and a little later the one that was placed to the right of the lift tower.

The tower stands fifteen meters tall and forms the only entrance to the house. The little cypress we planted at the end of the nineties, has now grown to be just over seven meters high. In other words, it's taken about 20 years to reach half the height of the lift tower. If it follows the same growth pattern in the years to come, it will most probably be our grandchildren who one day will find it interesting to pass by to see if it has managed to reach the top, or maybe even grown past the top of the tower.

It's about ten years since we moved from the house, but the memories from the time we planted that special cypress beside the lift tower, will never disappear.

Olivetti was an important office machine factory at the time.
Max Manus was their general agent in Norway from 1953 to 1967.

COINCIDENCES

2016

How in the world can it be that something as important as coincidences has not yet got its own reflection? The headline was written down a couple of years ago, and these days in 2018, I put the finishing touches to my book WORDS FOR THE ROAD - 114 short reflections, which I, without having this reflection in mind, dedicated to the "Coincidences".

Presumably, it's not common for a book to be dedicated to something so abstract or in this context remote.

As you can see, "Coincidences" is dated 2016. A series of coincidences have happened since then, but probably I have not been motivated to seize them and put them to paper. There may have been so many of them that I found it difficult to get started.

Why I chose this episode is pure coincidence, and that it happened during a period with a lot of stress, may be one of the reasons.

The choice between going on the train journey that would mark the celebration of our twenty years of marriage, or not, fortunately became quite easy. We had ordered the tickets a long time before my wife, three months ago suffered a stroke. To make a long story short, it fortunately seems to be going the right way and we are now at the convalescent stage. The doctors gave us the green light to travel as long as the medicine was taken and if my wife, of course, was motivated for the trip.

The last coincidence happened on June 14th. 2018, the

day before we went on our big train ride with "Al Andalus" through Extremadura.

The burglar alarm had broken down the day before and we needed urgent service not to leave the apartment unprotected. Of course, there was a lot of time-related stress, but it all worked out in the end, just hours before we left.

The same evening, we were to fly from Almeria to Seville late in the afternoon of the 15th., I discovered that my Omega watch had stopped. Strange, had the battery burned out? My wife was certain that it had been changed in Oslo while we were there last August. According to me it must have been two years ago, but that discussion we wisely avoided.

Here good advice was hard to come by. You cannot change the battery on an Omega just anywhere and especially not in the area where we live.

Friday and market day in Garrucha. An enormous amount of people, as the holiday season has already begun and as usual there are no parking spaces available. My wife, who cannot yet drive the car after her stroke, had a session of "radio frequency" in Garrucha, so after taking her to Liliana's, I finally found a parking space and walked confidently to the store that I thought had changed the battery the time before it was done in Oslo.

As it was market day, I found the door locked - it was clear that the owner did not see any business opportunities in keeping open on market days.

It's not that I'm without watches. In the safe I have a Callaway I got as a prize in a golf tournament, a Swatch that I don't remember the origins of and a self-winding Rado. I had all of them, including the Omega, in my pocket, as it should at least, I thought, be possible to revive one of them. The absence of a watch on a week's journey was unthinkable, especially due to our present situation with the state of health my wife is in, as her watch is non-numeric, resulting in her getting the hour wrong one way or the other, when I ask her what time it is. So, the last resort would be to buy a new one. With the door locked at the only shop I could imagine having the possibility of a battery change, I walked crestfallen through the small streets back towards the parking lot down by the harbour.

As I come out of a narrow street to cross Garrucha's seaside promenade, I suddenly see my Irish friend Allan, with his cap and his little backpack. He is one of those people who have walked the so-called pilgrimage to Santiago de Compostela from different starting points and is a very nice fellow whom we have known for many years.

I tell him about the stress factor over the last few days, our train ride and the present condition of my wife, ending with a quick resume of my watch experience.

First you go back less than fifty meters, then walk about a hundred meters to the right, he explains. On the left side corner there is a goldsmith shop whose proprietor is a watch specialist. According to Allan, who lives in Garrucha, he should be open on market days.

And sure enough, he was open. Nothing he could do about the Omega though, nor with the Rado's mechanics as they were far beyond his field of expertise. But when it came to changing batteries in the other two, he nodded with a smile.

Half an hour later I fetched the Callaway and the Swatch, both with new fresh batteries. As I had promised Allan to call him to tell him about the outcome, I, of course, did so immediately after picking up my wife from her treatment at Lilina's.

With Allan's good wishes for a nice trip, I hurried home to load our suitcases into the car.

Everything ready for the trip.

On our way along the motorway to Alicante, my wife discretely asked if it was not from Almeria we were going to fly? The airport in Alicante is a two-hour drive from us, in the opposite direction to the airport in Almeria, which we nomally reach in about three quarters of an hour.

Is it necessary to mention that the question, without any comment from my side, was answered by my taking the quickest exit to the right, and stopping at an appropriate spot to check the tickets. Minutes later we find ourselves heading in the opposite direction, on the motorway towards Almeria.

Stress, as there has naturally been a lot of lately, can have many consequences. By pure chance this misunderstanding on my part would save us from the consequence of another blunder I was responsible for.

After about twenty minutes driving towards Almeria, where I concentrated on checking my brain for other blunders, I discovered that maybe the most essential item apart from medicine, tickets and money, was well ensconced in the night-stand drawer at home.

The most important thing about my wife's rehabilitation is, of course, her medication. It is crucial for controlling her blood pressure, which should be measured twice daily. And how do you check the blood pressure? Quite right, you need a blood pressure gauge. Imagine how safe ours was at home in the night-stand drawer, protected by a well-functioning burglar alarm.

Thanks to the distance to Almeria being shorter compared to Alicante, we had time to drive into the city itself where we immediately found a pharmacy and bought the indispensable instrument.

It wasn't a coincidence that only after we checked in at the Almeria airport, we got communication going again.

THE WILL

May 2014

Unlike physical strength, I see the human will as an unbelievably strong resource. A strong-willed person often gets called that just because he is known for having a strong will. First we must clear away the will related to stubbornness, the one occurring specially in kids and adolescents.

Not that this type of will necessarily disappears because of one has grown up, but for those that applies to there will always be problems.

The will I have in mind is the positive will, the one that makes thoughts and meanings grow to new heights. The will to understand is one of several good examples of the positive will. You may as well call it the ground-breaking will.

If one is to reach a goal one has set for oneself, of whatever character, the will must be there.

It's not at all so that if only the will is there one automatically reaches all the goals one has set for oneself.

The will is only one of the ingredients needed to do so, but maybe the one that at the end of the day is the condition needed to put one's thoughts and meanings forward.

Back to the positive will, the will to understand.

For me it's totally clear that no challenges can be overcome if one doesn't have the will to do so, and if one wants to be able to overcome them, one has to understand both them and those involved.

One's will is a power which, when properly used, is incredibly strong.

People glowing of positive willpower normally have their understanding in order.

But, and that is important, it must be a positive, natural will and not one which is forced.

The will in itself can, in some, be destructive and effacing if seen in conjunction with negativity – negative will.

In this context it is a matter of people with weak willpower, or people with no will. No positivity can come from having weak willpower or being without a will.

I have little experience of how these expressions are used in daily life, but presume that they are quite similar when it comes to performance, although they are of different gravity.

If one has week willpower, the will still plays a role, although minor. If one on the contrary is without will, it means that one is devoid of will. In this case one is badly off for action.

When it comes to will and understanding, the weak-willed person will be poorly off in terms of understanding, while the ones without any will, will be devoid of that property.

Anyhow, all this is, of course, just a lot of theory. How the will is perceived by each one of us in our daily life, remains something we do not care to dwell on too often.

There are plenty of other things our brain must cope with.

> *The will to understand as well as the desire and belief that one will succeed, is a condition for reaching one's goals.*

> *The will to understand is fundamental. If one's will-power fails for lack of understanding, the result will be halting.*

PERTURBED

December 2018

Without going into more details about our morning routines, I only mention that the idea I got for this reflection came from my wife. This happened after the morning tee was served in bed and that we as usual on Saturdays have switched on the Spanish TV2 channel. Classical music in all categories starts the day. Today, it's a Spanish symphony orchestra having embarked on Robert Schumann -1810-1856.

Not quite our genre, but we stayed on the channel as we got to experience a special "percussionist", a drummer, who handled several instruments that none of us had seen before. The actual piece of music they performed, none of us had the great sense of.

Suddenly, my wife exclaims that Schumann did not have an easy time and further on that he was "perturber" or "perturbed".

Completely without understanding I ask what she means. As she is Swiss and I Norwegian and we between us communicate in English, it happens every now and then that unresolved phrases between us must be clarified. Her vocabulary in English is far better than mine, so normally it is me asking her to explain herself.

She briefly exclaims that Schumann was "perturber". My immediate question was what she meant by that, as I had never heard the word. French for "perturbed", she further explained, not making me much wiser. Yes, Schumann suffered from mental problems, she said, and she thought that an English word for it, however not often used, could be that: he was "perturbed".

The dialogue went a little back and forth to find a covering, and for us both understandable definition of the word. After all, she had expressed what she meant, so it became me who continued the exploration.

A good idea, I thought, would be to make a search on Google, took the tea cup and sat in front of the PC.

I became no wiser when I tried in Norwegian. First with "perturbed", which was translated into Norwegian as "opprørt". When I tried to find out what "opprørt" was in English, I was presented with upset. At some point in my amateurish way of searching, I had come across the word disturbed, which I thought might be correct, in the sense of mentally disturbed, not being disturbed in the sense interrupted. Disturbed was translated into disrupted and confirmed the other way, disrupted = disturbed. At this point It came to my mind that I would choose the word "forstyrret" - disturbed, if it was about desolation, and when that was checked, "forstyrret" - disturbed was translated as disturbed. I also tried to see if it could have anything to do with being confused and got an explanation that it could have something to do with being disoriented and or upset. So close but still not correct.

Long story short, I didn't get on. Humiliated I had to ask her for help.

First she consults The Oxford Guide to the English Language from 1989. Here she finds "perturbed" explained as gravely troubled, after which she looks up in Petit Larousse's illustrations from 1978, where the meaning is described as disturbed greatly.

No doubt, we were getting closer. Finally, I got a real example, with a dispute, on my definition of communication:

The highest form of communication is the one that even the unconditional can use and enjoy.

CRISIS MAXIMIZATION

November 2018

A week ago, I received an email from a friend in Norway who wondered if we were affected by the major devastation in our nearest town, Garrucha, down to the Mediterranean, ten minutes' drive from where we live. The person in question had watched the news and seen that Garrucha had been severely affected by the heavy rainfall.

Admittedly, we had had a few hours of continuous heavy rain and since the earth had not seen water for many months, large amounts of it quickly formed in places otherwise being crush dry.

There is no day without us driving through Garrucha, where we in addition to shops also have our mailbox.

The heavy rainfall occurred late in the evening with both lightning and thunder and when we drove out of the urbanization next morning, the bridge over the small river passing through the golf course, and in which there normally is no water, was flooded. We couldn't see the bridge itself, but only the river having crossed its banks. We had to pass with water covering almost up to half the wheels. The same thing happens this time every year and as it normally lasts no more than one day, we don't count it as one of the big events.

After having bought the newspaper where we always buy it, we continued the few minutes it takes to Garrucha. As the city is only a few hundred meters wide, but in return almost two kilometres long bordering on the Mediterranean, the few hundred meters going inland is rising from sea level to somewhere around fifty meters. Because of that, the streets going inland become rivers during heavy rainfall. That was what happened the night before.

We drove the seafront which we always do when we check out the mailbox. The post office is situated in the first quarter from the seafront.

Immediately we noticed that where all the crossroads end up at the seafront, some sand and gravel had been gathered, as everything loose in the streets during the rainy night had been washed down towards the seafront. Otherwise we saw no signs of destruction of any kind and everything seemed to be at its normal.

If this qualifies for the big news releases on Norwegian TV, the reporters must have few disastrous reports available.

"Fake news" has, of course, existed since endless times, but has been heavily actualized after Donald Trump's entry into politics.

Those not being aware that we daily are presented with large amounts of so-called "Fake news", can't possibly be observant when they acquire news, be it both written and pictorial.

Of course, it's just natural that news reports on TV presents the worst and most scaring examples available, as that's what they compete about in those circles - to be first with reports about what viewers want to see. It's probably little doubt that most of us choose the channels that usually present the worst situations.

It's rare, if it at all happens, that one is informed about the fact that the situation presented is the worst and perhaps the only one. The media has done nothing criminal by failing to inform us about the fact that in the big context it's the worst examples they focused upon.

Crisis maximization is also not uncommon in another context.

Personally, I tend to evoke the worst imaginable when something happens. Presumably, it's a hidden way of being prepared. Others probably have the opposite reaction, which is to see it from the angle that it's certainly not so serious.

ABOUT OPINIONS AND HAVING RIGHT

November 2018

In the past, it was important to me that people perceived what I meant about different topics. It was also important for me to emphasize what I thought was essential in the massage, to ensure I was understood.

The meaning was well meant from my side, but I often think that a lot of time was wasted. I was rightly quoted to use too many words.

Many things change with age, or as I prefer to call it, maturity,

Maybe I wasn't clever enough conveying my messages, or to dominant in the way they were presented, as I often felt a lack of response. Another reason for that could of course also be that I expressed myself unclear.

As mentioned, the feedback I got, for reasons I in those days didn't find an answer to, was quite few.

Maybe I should have kept my opinions closer to my chest and not been so concerned with other's thoughts. They probably had more than enough daily challenges themselves and therefore enough with their own opinions.

In other words, "Everyone has sufficient challenges with their own opinions".

With lessons learned from these observations, one should be realistic to oneself.

It doesn't mean that one should focus on isolation or selfishness, but perhaps be a little reluctant to loudly express ones opinions about everything.

I think that after all, people in general are more interested in their own opinions than others. On the other hand, it's not good with those who constantly urge to express their opinions and push them forward to others.

It's, of course, important that one have opinions and that one don't ignore them. The very fact that different views can and should be tested is the strength of democracy. Freedom of speech has little meaning if not used.

In this context, the phrase "everyone is right from their assumptions" is important. Everyone gathers information and experience from different backgrounds and thus are "right from their assumptions".

Far from everyone thinks that it is so but should for their own sake dwell about it before they strike with counter-arguments trying to reverse the opinion of the opposition.

It is not so important always to be right. Most people think that if they have an opinion on a matter, it's of the utmost importance to convince the party they argue with that they are right. Counter-arguments usually lead to one defending one's opinions and doing everything possible to convince the opposite party that one is right.

Why is it so important for most of us to be right? It is as if we constantly must convince ourselves that it gives a gain to be right and that it's a defeat if one isn't right in a case.

Why not just swallow your pride, if that's how it feels when one admits that others are right, and simply learn from it.

Here we again are in contact with the phrase: "The truth is ...". When someone uses that phrase, they don't necessarily mean this literally. If they do, they reveal their own ignorance if they don't add: "in my opinion" before or after: "The truth is ...".

The truth appears to be correct for the person using the phrase but will always reflect his or her assumptions regarding the subject in question.

Word duels we get served in every context. When the meaning is clear, that it's a competition with winners and losers it's okay, but if not, who judges the outcome and chooses the winner? Again, it's a question about assumptions. Here we ignore quizzes, where at least in most cases it must be assumed that the answer is correct.

In the world of politics, it is a question of winning the arguments, it's a matter of the favour of voters. Where is the truth in this context?

Forget it, everyone forms the truth based on their assumptions.

"The truth is", or "the fact is", one often hears in political debates where all parties usually pretend to be those who indisputably possess the patent of being right or, which they often let shine through, that they represent the real truth.

Could it be possible that you as a listener or viewer are so unwise that you don't understand that here you must be on guard? Or is it that you take it for granted that the political party you sympathize with really is right? Presumably the latter is correct, because if that wasn't the case you would not have sympathized with them.

So far there is no owner to the patent on "the truth", and there will never be one, but that "everyone is right from their assumptions", all can claim without showing dishonesty.

SELF-ASSESSMENT AND SELF-CRITICISM

December 2018

Could it be possible that this topic came to me completely by itself, or was it triggered by something very special?

It doesn't matter. It's typically an example of something that has been lying and smouldering, which the subconscious has quietly worked with over time.

The tolerance has, of course, been put to the test for a long time and all forms of compromise at your disposal have also been nurtured.

If I don't immediately mention that a case or an opinion at least has two sides, or parties, and that I am conscious about it, anyone could say that this isn't an objective opinion, but a clearly subjective assessment.

Admit-tingly, when I feel pressured, I am not the easiest, but I at least have a willingness to try to build bridges.

The way one look at oneself or judge oneself may vary quite considerably, as we are all different.

Nevertheless, the main feature is that we generally add better qualities to ourselves, that we think we are a little better than we really are and that we have a clearer view of most things than most others.

Here it sprinkles with the fertilizer for self-preservation.

What about the self-criticism? Clearly most of us think we are self-critical. We generally don't like to be criticized, but if we criticize ourselves, it stays only between us and our own conscience.

No one gets to know where we really stand. It's a lot of good protection in that, and you are not so easily exposed.

Many find themselves in such a world. In that way they shield themselves from the outside, believing that everything is fine, and for them it is so. They often remain in their own world, find their place in the hierarchy and function perfectly in the whole.

There are areas where I think it's appropriate that one exercise some self-criticism, however, and that is related to one's behaviour in everyday life. Ask yourself if you are usually paying attention to others?

Think about it carefully, it's not a matter of covering a big field. From the moment you start the day to you go to bed, you encounter an infinity of situations where you deliberately or unconsciously leave a print of your personality. You are judged by others based on your actions and behaviour. If you attitude is that you do not care about it, you can't expect anything but general negativity to your own personality.

In this context, it's amazing how important the real smile is. A smile costs nothing but gives so much. Yes, I claim that it requires very little from your side to be perceived as a considerate human being.

Not that you in any way should expect someone to give you this in writing, but the guaranteed most valuable gain you can get is your own good feeling of knowing that you are generally a considerate human being.

Now, don't let this go to your head, you will have many negative feelings of not being perceived as the one you want to be, but it's not your problem if you are otherwise satisfied with the sincere attempt you have made to act more considerate in daily life.